0.99

D1467634

Romance at Rainbow's End

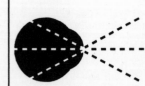

This Large Print Book carries the
Seal of Approval of N.A.V.H.

ROMANCE AT RAINBOW'S END

COLLEEN L. REECE

THORNDIKE PRESS
A part of Gale, Cengage Learning

GALE
CENGAGE Learning·

Detroit • New York • San Francisco • New Haven, Conn • Waterville, Maine • London

GALE
CENGAGE Learning®

Thorndike Press® Large Print Clean Reads.
The text of this Large Print edition is unabridged.
Other aspects of the book may vary from the original edition.
Set in 16 pt. Plantin.

LIBRARY OF CONGRESS CATALOGING-IN-PUBLICATION DATA

Reece, Colleen L.
    Romance at rainbow's end / by Colleen L. Reece. — Large print edition.
      pages ; cm. — (California brides series ; #3) (Thorndike Press large print clean reads)
    ISBN-13: 978-1-4104-6168-1 (hardcover)
    ISBN-10: 1-4104-6168-8 (hardcover)
    1. Large type books. I. Title.
PS3568.E3646R658 2013
813'.54—dc23   2013021471

Published in 2013 by arrangement with Barbour Publishing, Inc.

For Susan K. Marlow —
the story continues . . .

ONE

Angry voices drifted up to the loft of the shack the Stoddard family called home. They yanked eleven-year-old Ellianna out of a sound sleep. She shifted on the rustling cornhusk mattress and buried her head in her thin pillow. Hands clenched, she lay rigid, wanting to scream at Pa and Agatha to stop fighting.

A cold, skinny hand touched her hair. "Ellie? Are you awake?"

She opened her eyes. Timmy stood beside her, shivering in his thin nightdress. His frightened eyes looked enormous in the dim light that filtered through unpatched holes in the attic roof.

"Who can sleep in this racket?" She scooted over. "Crawl in before you freeze."

Timmy scrambled under the blanket and snuggled close. "Make them stop, Ellie."

"I can't." A pang went through her. Years of neglect and lack of love had toughened her, but her little brother shouldn't have to live with the likes of Gus and Agatha. *It's bad enough for me,* her heart protested, *but Timmy's only eight.*

A loud crash from below brought her bolt upright. Timmy's fingers dug into her arm. "What's that, Ellie?"

"Probably a chair turning over." She loosened his death grip. "Stay here. I'll find out." She slid to the floor, crept over to the opening at the top of the rickety ladder, and peered down. Agatha was shaking her fist in Pa's face.

Ellie sneered. When Pa had married Agatha two years earlier, the woman had been all smiles. "My name means 'kind and good,'" she'd gushed. "I just know we are all going to be a wonderful, happy family."

Ellie felt like throwing up. A few weeks after the honeymoon, *kind* and *good* gave way to screaming and stinging blows for the two youngest Stoddards. Agatha didn't dare hit Ian or Peter. At twelve and fourteen they were already nearly as tall as their father. Instead, Agatha made up lies about them that earned beatings from Gus. A few months ago, the boys had disappeared. Agatha pretended to be sorry, but Ellie overheard her mutter, "Good riddance."

Now Ellie held her breath and watched an ugly scowl cover her stepmother's face. "I've put up with your brats long enough," Agatha shrilled. "It's time for them to go."

Pa's black eyes narrowed to slits. "*Go?* You already drove Ian and Peter away."

Agatha snorted. "Gus Stoddard, you are such a hypocrite! If you cared one whit about your family, you wouldn't have left them to shift for themselves all those months while you were out West, trying to make your stepdaughter marry a gambler to pay your debts. If neighbors hadn't lent a hand, they'd have starved."

"And you've never let me forget it!" Gus spit out, his face an angry red. "Lay off me. It's none of your business how I handle my kids!"

Her raucous laugh brought him a step nearer, but she wasn't through. "It is my business. I got taken in with your butter-wouldn't-melt-in-your-mouth ways, just like your other two wives. They up and died on you, but I've no intention of dying. I've had enough of living in this shack with two worthless brats. You're going to get rid of them, stop drinking, get a job, and be respectable."

Not likely. Ellie covered her mouth to keep

back a laugh that turned into a silent sob. Childish voices, taunting and cruel, pounded in her brain: *You ain't nothing, Ellianna Stoddard. Neither's your Pa. Trash, that's what you are — and you ain't never gonna be nothin' else.*

Ellie cringed. Resentment toward her father, who had made her the target of jeering schoolmates, swelled until she found it hard to breathe. Then Agatha's voice sliced into her consciousness, cold and hard as an ice-covered rock:

"I mean it, Gus. Either ship Timmy and Ellie out West to that rich rancher Sarah married, or send them to the orphanage. I don't care which." She paused, then hissed, "Listen, and listen good. I want those kids out of here!"

Stunned by Agatha's viciousness, Ellie staggered back to bed. She found Timmy scrunched under the covers with his hands over his ears.

"What's happening, Ellie?" His voice trembled.

"Shhh. Go to sleep. I'm here." Yet after he fell asleep and silence reigned below, Ellie lay wide awake, glad for the warmth of her brother's frail body. What would tomorrow bring? And the day after that?

It can't be any worse than the past. Ellie

10

sighed. *I've never been more to Pa than just another mouth to feed. And since Sarah left, someone to do for him.* Her bitter thoughts rushed on. The only kindness she had ever known was when Gus married Virginia Anderson, a wonderful Christian woman. Virginia conscientiously cared for Ellie and her three brothers, along with her own teenagers, Seth and Sarah.

A lone tear slid from beneath Ellie's tightly closed eyelid, followed by rebellion. Two years after Virginia died, Sarah had slipped away in the night. Seth had already fled Gus's wrath. Their leaving made eight-year-old Ellie the woman of the house.

"It's not fair," she whispered, too low to disturb Timmy. "I did everything I could to please Pa and the boys. All I got were slaps and complaints when the food burned."

Powerless to stop the raging memories, Ellie thought of how she'd lived in fear when Gus was drinking or lost at gambling. The older boys took off, but she and Timmy hid. During the past three years of drudgery, she'd tried to remember what her step-mother had taught her about Jesus. Was there really such a Person? She sadly shook her head. No man of her acquaintance bore any resemblance to the kindly, loving Christ Virginia had described.

11

Shortly after Sarah fled, Pa had announced he and Tice Edwards were going to California to fetch her home. Ellie's poor, tired heart bounced. She and Sarah hadn't gotten along very well, but maybe things would be different now. If Sarah and Tice got married like Pa said, would they let her live with them? Or at least help out so Ellie didn't have to work so hard?

A second tear crawled out. Pa came home without Tice, blaming the gambler's death on Sarah's stubbornness and sourly saying she was going to marry a rancher. Now his threat was, "If you younguns don't behave, I'll ship you off to California and let the mountain lions eat you."

It struck terror into the already cowed children. Ellie continued to do as she was told, seldom spoke, and silently bore the shame of being Gus Stoddard's daughter. Although longing to learn, she secretly felt relieved when Pa ordered her to stay home and tend the house and Timmy. It meant temporary freedom from tormenting schoolmates who delighted in mocking her, leaving scars so deep she felt they would never heal.

What they said was true. She was nothing. Pa was nothing. And nothing would ever change. She'd go on day after endless

12

day cooking, scrubbing, and mending. When she was a little older, she'd be sent out as a laundress as Sarah had been. Ellie sighed. Was Sarah happy now that she was married? Or had a mountain lion eaten her?

One day, Pa had come in from the few days' work he did at a time on the St. Louis docks, just enough to keep the family from starving, and dropped into a chair. "Tomorrow you slick this place up, you hear? Ellie, make the best supper you can. Tim, help her." A self-conscious smirk crawled across his face, and he dropped into a rickety chair. "We're havin' comp'ny."

Company? Ellie didn't dare ask, but Timmy had no such qualms. "Who?"

Gus scowled. "Mrs. Batdorf, that's who. You're to mind your manners. She's a widow-lady I met at church.

"Church?" Ellie blinked. Pa hadn't gone to church since he'd married Virginia Anderson.

"Sure." Gus guffawed. "Best place there is to find good, hard-working wives."

Ellie sniffed, then brightened. Would Mrs. Batdorf be as nice as Virginia had been, even when the children didn't mind her?

"Do we have to call her Ma?" Timmy persisted.

Gus slapped him, then leaned back until

the tired chair screeched in protest. "You'll treat her with respect, or I'll send you to Seth and Sarah."

"To California? Where the mountain lions are?" Timmy wailed. "I don't wanna go, Pa. Please don't make us go!"

The chair came forward with a crash. "You'll do what I tell you, hear? Don't you forget: mountain lions have powerful big teeth and are mighty fierce."

Timmy cried himself to sleep that night . . . and a cold, hard knot that chilled Ellie through and through began to form in her breast.

The morning after Agatha's ultimatum dawned gray and cheerless. Breakfast was a disaster. The biscuits Ellie had learned to make light and fluffy didn't rise. Pa fired one at the wall. "Seems like a man should be able to have decent food around here."

Ellie didn't bother to tell him they had what he provided, but Agatha did. "Baking powder's probably too old. Time to change it — and other things."

Timmy's big brown eyes, so unlike Ellie's crystal blue ones, opened wide. "What's gonna change?" he asked.

Gus hesitated, then pulled a soiled sheet of paper from his pocket. Ellie noticed how he refused to look at them when he said, "I'm sending this telegram to Seth and Sarah this morning." He smoothed out the crumpled page and read:

REMARRIED *Stop* PETER AND IAN ON OWN *Stop* ELLIE AND TIMMY ARRIVE MADERA 23 *Stop*.

Even though she'd known it was coming, the words hit Ellie like a runaway freight train. She stared at Pa, who still avoided her gaze; at Agatha, swelled with triumph; and last of all, at her little brother's peaked, terrified face. Bile rose in her throat. She shoved back her chair, snatched Timmy by the hand, and dragged him away from the man who had betrayed his children.

"Git back over here," Gus ordered.

They had no choice but to obey. Ellie tightened her hold on her brother and returned to the table, vowing to protect Timmy as best she could. She sent Agatha a look of loathing and asked, "When do we go?"

Gus cleared his throat. "Today. If they don't want you, there'll be no time for them to say so."

Fear spurted. What if Seth and Sarah didn't want them? It was no secret Ellie and

Timmy had given Sarah plenty of grief. She still remembered snatching up Sarah's hand one time and biting it. She winced.

But Ellie couldn't think of that right now. She pushed her terror aside and dropped to her knees beside Timmy, who was sobbing uncontrollably. "God is going to pay you back for this," she told the two adults towering above her.

Agatha put on an aggrieved look. "Why, Ellianna! How can you speak so to me and to the father who loves you and knows best? Surely the stepmother I'm always hearing about must have taught you that children are to obey their parents in all things. The Bible says so."

Criticism of Virginia, who had tried to be a good mother in spite of Ellie's rebellion, overcame her fear. If she didn't speak out, she'd burst. She leaped to her feet. "How dare you quote the Bible to me? *You're* making Pa send us away. I heard you shrieking at him last night." Her voice became a perfect imitation of Agatha's:

" 'I've had enough of living in this shack with two worthless brats. You're going to get rid of them, stop drinking, get a job, and be respectable.' "

"You ungrateful girl! What if I did?" Agatha thrust her mottled face close to Ellie's.

"No one wants the likes of you around. They never will. If Sarah takes you in, which she may not, it will be from pity and duty, not love."

Ellie's tongue cleaved to the roof of her mouth, and her heart felt like lead. What if Agatha was right? She felt Timmy tug at her worn, calico gown. Tears streaked his dirty face.

"Won't they want us, Ellie?"

"Don't be foolish. Of course they will," she soothed. But the question hammered at her brain until she thought it would burst.

A few hours later, Ellie and Timmy stood beside the train that would carry them to California. Timmy screamed again that he didn't want to go, but Gus shook the daylights out of him, turned without so much as a *Godspeed,* and walked away.

In that moment, the meekness behind which Ellie had always masked her feelings for her father turned to hatred. She put a comforting arm around her brother and led him up the train steps. The conductor took them to their seats, and Timmy snuggled down next to her, crying as if his heart would break. "Don't worry, Timmy. I'll take care of you. So will Seth and Sarah. They live on a big ranch, remember? It will be lots of fun. Why, I'll bet they'll even have a pony you can ride."

"You won't let a mountain lion get me?" Timmy quavered.

"No." Feeling years older than she actually was, Ellie gently laid his head in her lap and stared out the train window. But she didn't see the scenery through which they were traveling. What would California be like? Would Sarah and Seth — and that rancher-fellow, what was his name? Matt? — be sorry that she and Timmy had come? A lifetime of misery swept through her. *Jesus, if You are really like stepmama said, please . . .*

She couldn't continue, but a small, comforting thought came: No matter what lay ahead, she and Timmy were free from Gus and Agatha.

Two

Spring 1892
San Francisco
The *rat-a-tat-tat* of knuckles against the ornate door of Joshua Stanhope's study at Bayview Christian Church yanked him from his concentration. He flung down his fountain pen and muttered something more annoyed than elegant. *Of all the rotten luck!*

After struggling all morning with Sunday's sermon, his train of thought had finally gotten on track. Why did he have to be derailed just when he was finally forging full steam ahead? The knocking came again. Louder, and not to be ignored.

Josh heaved a sigh. "Come in."

The door swung open. "Hey, Reverend, who do you know in Madera?" a laughing voice demanded.

Josh stared at his mirror image. Same six-foot height. Same lean build. Same gray eyes and short blond hair, except every hair on Edward's head was in place. Josh grimaced, knowing his own locks must bear evidence of his running his fingers through them while trying to solve knotty problems.

"Well?" Edward persisted.

"No one. And don't call me Reverend."

Edward donned an innocent expression that didn't fool Josh one bit. "You *are* a minister, remember?" He smirked. "Besides, doesn't the Bible tell us to respect our elders? This means that since you're five minutes older than I am, you're the big brother."

Josh winced. He loved his twin more than life itself but wished Edward wouldn't take things so lightly. "Why the sudden interest in Madera?"

Edward handed him a letter. "Your secretary gave it to me when I told him I had to see you on a matter of life or death."

"Life or death?" Josh raised a skeptical eyebrow. "You look pretty healthy to me."

Edward slumped into the massive chair across from his brother. "Beryl will kill me if I'm late for lunch. That fiancée of mine is a stickler for being on time, so I dropped by to see if I could get a loan. Believe it or not, Dad's playing the heavy-handed father. He wouldn't give me an advance, and Mother's off at some do-gooder meeting." He scowled. "Why'd Grandpa have to tie up the principal of what he left us until we're thirty? I could use the cash now, not three years from now."

Josh gritted his teeth. "I manage all right."

Edward hooted. "*You* have a fat salary. Even if you didn't, don't forget John the Baptist. Preachers aren't supposed to have a lot of money. So . . . I'm here to relieve you of some of yours."

Josh knew he shouldn't encourage Edward by laughing, but he couldn't help it. Indolent, always out for a good time, Edward Stanhope possessed a sunny personality few could resist. "Why can't you take life seriously?"

"Moi?" Edward's eyes twinkled. "No thanks."

A familiar ache attacked Josh's breastbone. *Why, Lord? I'm giving my life to serving You, but I can't show my own brother how much he needs You.*

Edward stood and stretched like a lazy cat. "Aren't you going to open your letter? On the other hand, why bother? It's probably someone asking for money. Hey, while we're on the subject, how about that loan?"

A strange reluctance to open the letter in Edward's presence caused Josh to reach for his pocketbook and hand Edward a few

21

crumpled bills.

"Thanks, old man. You'll get it back the first of next month. *Au revoir.*" He sent Josh a brilliant smile and hurried out the door, closing it behind him.

The young minister dropped his head into his hands. Most encounters with Edward left him feeling frustrated and helpless to change his twin's carefree ways. Five minutes in their birth order had made him the elder brother, but Josh's relationship with the Lord cast him in a brother's-keeper role he often felt inadequate to play.

"It's not that Edward doesn't believe in You," Josh prayed. "He does, but it isn't enough to make a real difference in his life." He sighed. "Once Edward marries Beryl Westfield, there's even less chance of him ever having a real relationship with You."

An image of the haughty, dark-haired woman flickered into Josh's mind. Five years older than the twins and a self-proclaimed infidel, Beryl had unsuccessfully pursued Josh before turning her charms on Edward. Josh tolerated her for his brother's sake but considered her a threat to his and Edward's close relationship.

Feeling like Atlas forever trying to hold up the sky, Josh slid to his knees, one hand resting on his highly polished desk. "Lord, how many times have I given Edward over to You, then snatched him back? Help me remember that You love him even more than I do and are in control." After a long time, he raised himself with one hand, feeling a measure of peace. The forgotten letter rustled, reminding him it needed to be read. Josh sat down again and opened it. His gray gaze riveted on the scrawled first line: *You may not remember me, but you saved my life nine years ago.*

Who on earth . . . ? Josh quickly looked at the bottom of the page. The signature sent shock ripples through him — *Red Fallon.* The letter fell to the desk from nerveless fingers. Remember! How could he forget?

Josh closed his eyes. In a heartbeat, he was eighteen again, hurrying through a dark alley on one of San Francisco's meanest streets — a place he'd been strictly forbidden to go. He could see the expensively furnished drawing room in the Stanhope Nob Hill mansion and his mother's face a few hours earlier. . . .

Jewels sparkled on Mother's hands, and she held them up in shocked protest. "No son of mine is going to be part of some so-called rescue mission! It doesn't matter that your uncle runs it. It isn't fitting. No gentleman would be caught dead down there with a bunch of criminals and the scum of the earth! That's what you'll be if you try to follow in Marvin's footsteps — dead."

Josh didn't argue. He just waited until the mansion lay silent and sneaked out. Guilt dogged every step of the way to the mission, but something greater than the "honour thy father and mother" commandment he'd learned as a child compelled him to continue. He reached his destination without mishap and decided to enter through the door behind the mission. If a Stanhope servant had seen Josh slip out and reported him, Mother would already have sent a carriage to "rescue" him.

He held his breath and groped his way down the dark alley. A short way from the mission door, he stumbled and nearly fell. His hands shot down to regain his balance — and encountered rough material.

Horrified at the contact, Josh forced himself not to run. "God, help me!" he whispered. Strength beyond description surged through him. He gritted his teeth, picked up the inert body that lay at his feet, and stumbled his way to the mission door. He gave it a hard kick and cried, "Uncle Marvin! Help!"

The door swung out and back. A tall man pulled Josh inside. He slammed and bolted the door, then relieved Josh of his burden. He laid the lifeless body on a nearby cot and bent over to examine it. "What are you doing here, Joshua?"

The stiffening in Josh's knees gave way. He sank into a chair. "I don't know. I just felt I had to come." He peered at the man on the cot. Dark stains matted the red hair, and dried blood nearly covered the craggy face. "Is he" — Josh choked — "is he dead?"

"Almost. Son, if you hadn't found him when you did, this man — whoever he is — would be a goner." Marvin shook his head. "He still may not make it. . . ."

Josh wiped a hand across his eyes and erased the scene from his past. It did not erase the hard beating of his heart. Or the memory of what followed that terrible night at the mission. God had once again been merciful to a sinner: a wild cowboy who had been beaten almost to death. Josh thought of how he'd sneaked away from home as often as he could without being detected. He'd hated deceiving his parents but had recognized much more than obedience to his parents hung on what was happening at the mission.

Now he bowed his head. Gratitude raced through him. "Lord, 'soup, soap, and salvation' healed Red Fallon's body, mind, and soul." A lump rose to Josh's throat. That fateful night had also irrevocably changed his own life. Watching God work through Uncle Marvin as he cared for Red Fallon had set a blaze burning in Josh's soul that had never died.

He picked up the letter again. Except for a few sporadic notes from Red over the years, they'd lost touch. Why was he writing now? The further Josh read, the more he marveled. Red wrote:

It took a heap of time for folks here in Madera — especially Abby Sheridan, the prettiest little filly in the valley — to believe I'd really changed. They finally did. So did Abby. Now we're married with a couple of little cowpunchers.

I been tryin to tell others about Jesus. There's a lot of cowhands just like me who oughta grab hold of Him. A few are willin to listen. I guess they figger if God could forgive the likes of me after all the bad I did, He could save most anybody.

The minister here's leavin in a few months. I hear tell you're some punkins at that big city church, but it don't cost nothin to ask: Will you come to Madera? We need you. Bad.

Josh stared at the final words until they blurred, then looked around the tastefully decorated study and out the window that overlooked San Francisco Bay. Lazy, white waves ruffled the shore. A horse-drawn carriage rumbled over the cobblestone street. The mournful cry of a ferryboat in the distance slowly dwindled into silence.

Josh took in a long breath, held it, then slowly released it. He'd come a long way since that night in the alley. Not just blocks away from the mission, but to Bayview Christian. High atop a hill with an incomparable view, the church was one of the most imposing and respected in the city. Filling the pulpit meant the height of San Francisco success for any minister, especially one as young as Josh.

Why then should Red's letter fill him with emotions he couldn't understand? What had a plea from a rescued cowboy who was *"tryin to tell others about Jesus"* and needed help *"bad"* to do with Joshua Stanhope?

THREE

Dozens of sparkling prisms hanging from a large chandelier reflected off Letitia Stanhope's diamond necklace and set rainbows dancing around the large dining room. Correct in the formal attire his mother insisted on for dinner, Joshua forked his Lady Baltimore cake into infinitesimal pieces and ignored the table conversation.

Edward's mocking voice interrupted Josh's woolgathering. "So, Reverend, what did your letter from Madera want? Money, I'll wager."

For once, Josh didn't tell his brother not to call him *Reverend.* Instead, the first words that came to mind popped out, "Not money. Me." The next instant, he wished he could crawl under the table — anything to get away from the accusing faces turned toward him.

"What?" Edward's eyebrows shot up.

Mother gasped and dropped her silver

fork to the damask table covering. A red tide rose from her lace collar to her carefully coiffed blond hair. She opened her mouth to speak, but Charles forestalled her. Josh caught his father's significant glance at Maria, the maid who helped serve and now stood frozen beside his chair.

"We will discuss it later." The finality in his announcement offered Josh a temporary reprieve but didn't erase his regret. Why had he blurted out the last thing he should have said? His mother's expression warned of an impending storm. Josh dreaded the session that would surely be as relentless as the gale-force waves that sometimes beat against the rocky shore of San Francisco Bay.

If only he could get away for a few moments to collect his wits before the family left the dining room! Josh glanced around the table, looking for a way to escape. His gaze stopped at his crystal water goblet. He raised it to his lips, then jerked his arm. Water cascaded down the front of his waistcoat and dripped onto the table. He snatched his linen napkin and began mopping up. "Sorry."

"Of all the awkward — let Maria do that and go change your clothes," Mother ordered. "Don't dawdle. We'll wait for you in the library."

"Yes, Mother." Josh stood. But before leaving the room, he saw Edward's eyes narrow. Josh sighed. Fooling his mother was one thing. Putting anything over on his twin was almost impossible. Well, at least the diversion had given him a few moments alone before facing his family.

Josh changed into dry clothes and knelt beside his heirloom bed. "Lord, why am I feeling so defensive? It's not like I'm going to Madera."

"Oh?"

The unspoken word left Josh gasping. He tried to laugh off his reaction but failed miserably. "Surely You don't mean for me to leave San Francisco," he prayed, trying to ignore his rapidly beating heart. "Not when everything is going so well at Bayview Christian." Yet doubt niggled. What if God meant just that? Josh shook his head, remembering the tempest that had followed his decision to go into the ministry nine years earlier. A tempest so strong it almost tore his family apart.

Josh's mind flashed back to the day he'd chosen God's path instead of the path his parents — especially his mother — had selected. His heart thundered, just as it had on that long-ago day. He'd honored his father and mother since childhood, but he *could* not, *would* not deny his Master's call — even if it meant alienation from his family. After rescuing Red Fallon, the call had grown from a spark to a living flame, fueled by stories from the Bible of those who left all to follow God . . . most of all, Joshua's challenge to the Israelites: *"Choose you this day whom ye will serve . . . : but as for me and my house, we will serve the Lord."*

Josh had thrilled to the words that had extinguished any lingering doubts. Then he'd girded himself for battle and shattered the silence of the quiet library with his announcement.

"Mother, Dad, I don't want to disappoint you, but I'm not going to be a 'doctor, lawyer, merchant, or chief,' as the old saying goes." His parents and Edward sat like statues. Only the crackle of the fire broke the stillness. Josh licked his dry lips and added, "God is calling me to be a minister."

Josh recalled the bitter scene that followed, but warmed at the memory of how Edward had defended him.

"Don't get upset, Mother," he'd said. "The last I heard, the ministry was still a respectable profession." Edward flashed the winning smile that seldom failed to get him what he wanted. "Think how proud you'll be when the *San Francisco Chronicle* reports, 'Reverend Joshua Stanhope, son of Charles and Letitia Stanhope, continues to fill the pews of First Church, or Bayview Christian, or one of the other leading churches with his powerful preaching and persuasive personality.' "

Mother hadn't been convinced. "But what will our friends think?"

"Letitia, our friends will be happy for us or kind enough to mind their own business," Father had said. "I'm proud that one of our sons is choosing to follow his heart."

Mother immediately ruffled her feathers on Edward's behalf. "Don't be so judgmental, Charles. Edward's music is just as important as Joshua wanting to preach."

"Hardly." Edward stood and stretched. "It might be different if I thought God wanted me to do something important with my music."

"You may find out if you take the time to listen," Josh told him. "Remember what happened to the man in the Bible who buried his talent?"

"Of course I remember. God called him a wicked and slothful servant." Edward grinned and clasped his hands behind his head. "I won't forget what our Sunday school teacher said when I asked her to explain *slothful.*" He pursed his lips and raised his voice to a high treble. " 'A sloth is one of the ugliest animals ever created and by far the laziest.' "

The corners of Mother's mouth turned down. "You aren't slothful. You just haven't decided what you want to do with your life. It's probably best, considering what Joshua is planning."

Edward shrugged. "Let him go ahead and become a preacher. If he doesn't like it, he can always be something else." Mischief danced in his eyes. "Maybe someday Josh can convert me."

Josh recoiled, as he always did when his brother treated eternal issues lightly. "Only God can do that."

"I know."

But after the family meeting ended, Edward had gone to his brother's room. "Sorry for being flippant, old man. The truth is, we're so much alike, I'm afraid if I ever get serious about religion, God might want more of me than I can give." He strode off, leaving Josh speechless and praying for his unpredictable twin.

Josh's thoughts returned to the present. Still on his knees, he sought out his heavenly Father. "Lord, give me a quiet spirit and the right words when I go downstairs. The idea of my going to Madera will send my family into turmoil. Mother found it nearly impossible to swallow when I became a minister. If You call me to preach to cowboys and ranchers, she'll feel it's beyond the pale."

A scripture that had sustained Josh in his revolt nine years earlier rushed into his mind: *"Then said Jesus unto his disciples, If any man will come after me, let him deny himself, and take up his cross, and follow me."*

Did "taking up his cross and following" mean losing Mother and possibly Edward? Dad might not agree with his son's decision, but he would never forsake him. Neither would God. Taking a deep breath, Josh got to his feet and slowly went downstairs.

Mother's first words showed she was primed for battle. "What did you mean about someone in Madera wanting you? Who is this person? How dare he approach you?" She broke her staccato questions to add, "I presume it's a he. Or is some brazen girl or woman attempting to lure you to that godforsaken place?"

Josh quelled the desire to laugh. "Not a girl or woman. A man I once helped."

Mother pounced. "Helped? Who? How? When? Where? Why do I know nothing of this?" She sniffed. "Really, Joshua, sometimes you are so quixotic. Helping a person doesn't give him a claim on you. Why can't you be more like Edward?"

Josh winced. If only Mother would accept him as he was. "Why are you getting upset over something that may never happen? The letter simply asks if I'd be willing to come to Madera. The pastor of the church is leaving, and —"

"Go to Madera?" Mother shrilled. "Leave San Francisco and Bayview Christian? Is this person a lunatic?"

Josh's hopes of making her understand died aborning. "No." What would she think if he repeated parts of Red's letter, words that had indelibly etched themselves into his brain: *Will you come to Madera? We need you. Bad.*

How Mother and Edward would jeer! The minister of the most prestigious church in San Francisco summoned to a cow town by an illiterate ne'er-do-well? It was almost more than even Josh could comprehend, yet a flutter of anticipation stirred inside him. What if God was using Red Fallon to carry out His purposes in Madera — and in Josh's life?

The family meeting continued amid protests from his mother that cut Josh to the heart. She ended with a final thrust. "We

35

had this discussion nine years ago, Joshua. I gave in to your whims. I admit things have turned out better than I ever expected. However, if you even consider this outrageous proposition, there will be consequences." She swept out of the library.

When Josh closed his bedroom door for the night, he couldn't shut out the feeling that he stood at a crossroads. For the second time that day, he knelt beside his bed. "Father, my heart feels heavy enough to crush my chest. Please give me peace." He waited. Instead of peace, conviction came. He owed it to God to take Red's plea seriously.

"Lord, I need to know if this is Your will. It means bucking Mother, but I'll contact Red and see if the church board wants me to come preach. If they do, I'll arrange for a leave of absence and go to Madera . . . then leave the future in Your hands."

Once in bed, Josh stared out his open window at the starless sky until his vision blurred. He fell asleep with Red's words echoing in his heart.

We need you. Bad.

How long had it been since anyone at Bayview Christian had spoken those words?

FOUR

June 1892
Madera, California

Ellie halted her paint mare beneath a huge oak tree on the wide promontory overlooking the Diamond S Ranch. She slid from the saddle and dropped the reins. Trained to being ground tied, Calico nosed Ellie's shoulder then found a sparse patch of grass and began to graze. Ellie walked to the large boulder where she had spent many happy hours and sat down. Her heart swelled. She never tired of the view. She never would. Not if she lived on the ranch seventy years instead of the seven she'd already been there.

She flung off her sombrero and ran a hand through her hair. Thank goodness it had finally grown long enough to turn under at the nape of her neck! Ellie remembered sobbing when she recovered enough from pneumonia to comprehend she'd been shorn like a lamb.

"Young lady, you don't realize how sick you've been. Sick and out of your head a lot of the time," Doc Brown had told her. "Any doctor worth his salt orders long, heavy hair to be cut in severe cases of pneumonia."

His explanation didn't console Ellie for losing her dark tresses. "I don't see how cutting a person's hair can help."

"Well, it does," he said. "High fever and the hair's weight sap a patient's energy." Doc's voice softened. "We were doing everything we could to save your life, Ellie."

Now she whispered, "Thank You, Lord, for sparing me. I'm just happy to be alive." She turned her attention to her surroundings. Could any spot on earth be lovelier? The rocky outcropping high above the Sterling ranch offered a bird's-eye view of rangeland, vineyards, orchards, and the San Joaquin River. Nothing disturbed Ellie's solitude except an eagle circling in the sky and the bawling of cattle far below. She laughed and tried to pick out Timmy from among the riders tending the herd. "Oops. He's Tim, not Timmy now," she told Calico. No wonder. At fifteen, her brother topped her five-foot-six inches by half a foot.

Ellie flung her arms to the sky, heart bursting with joy. "Thank You, God!" she cried, feeling as free as the eagle above her. She'd never dreamed she could be this happy. She reveled in the moment, wishing she could hug it to her heart and keep it there forever. But when a cloud drifted across the sun and cast a shadow over the smiling land, she stared unseeingly into the valley.

"Seven years, Lord. So much has happened! And much more to come." She drew her knees to her chest and laughed. "Including the fiesta." Excitement spurted through her. Needing someone with whom to share her excitement, Ellie glanced at Calico. Long experience had shown the mare to be a safe confidante.

"Folks from Madera and the neighboring ranches will come this afternoon for games and races and a barbecue supper."

Calico stopped grazing and looked mildly interested. Ellie continued.

"It's so hard to believe all the hustle and bustle at the ranch is for me! It's Solita's doing, you know." She pictured the Sterlings' diminutive Mexican housekeeper. Solita had planted her hands on her apron-covered hips in the spotless ranch house kitchen and announced in a voice that brooked no opposition, "*Senorita* Ellie will only have one eighteenth birthday. We will make *una gran fiesta* for her, *Senor* Mateo."

Ellie chuckled. Matt Sterling might own the Diamond S, but Solita ruled him and everyone else with a kind but unyielding hand.

Drifting shadows reminded Ellie she wasn't accomplishing the purpose for which she'd ducked out on the fiesta preparations and ridden to the promontory. A sigh started at her toes and crawled up. Where should she begin her journey from the past? At the St. Louis station when her father put her and Timmy on the westbound train and turned away without a backward glance?

"No!" Ellie shivered in spite of the warm day. She wrapped her arms more tightly around herself. Reliving that moment brought back feelings better left buried. Only then could she hold back the bitterness toward Gus Stoddard that lingered after all these years. "I'll start with when we arrived in Madera. . . ."

Heart beating double time, eleven-year-old Ellie took Timmy by the hand and slowly stepped down from the train, hating to leave the frail security it had afforded on the long journey west. *What if Sarah and Seth don't want us?*

A welcoming voice called, "Where are Ellie and Timmy?" The next moment, Ellie

40

was in Sarah's arms, with Seth lifting Timmy off his feet and swinging him around in a circle.

"Thought you'd never get here, old man," Seth said.

"Where are the mountain lions?"

Ellie caught the fearful glance Timmy sent around the station.

Seth looked puzzled. "Up in the mountains where they belong. What made you think we have mountain lions in Madera?"

Timmy bit his lip. Ellie suspected it was to hide its trembling. "Pa said if we didn't mind, he'd send us out here and we'd get eaten up by mountain lions."

"I told him I wouldn't let it happen," Ellie put in.

"We won't, either," Sarah promised. "You may never even see a mountain lion. Now, get in the buggy so we can go home. It's ten miles, and it looks like rain. We got more than our fair share this past February, and it looks like a few more drops might be headed this way." She laughed. "I like a sprinkle now and again, but it's nicer being inside looking out than outside when it pours!"

The tight knot in Ellie's chest loosened. It didn't sound like Sarah and Seth were angry with Pa for sending her and Timmy. She

41

climbed into the buggy. Sarah took her hand, and Ellie gradually relaxed against her stepsister's shoulder. Soon the *pitter-patter* of raindrops on the top of the buggy lulled her to sleep.

A gentle shake awakened Ellie. How different from Gus's usual bellow: *"Git up, Girl. There's work to be done!"*

Ellie slowly opened her eyes. She blinked. The sun had come out over a distant hill. Its rays mingled with the light rain and produced the most beautiful rainbow Ellie had ever seen. It arched the sky, and one end rested on a hacienda-style ranch house. Yet the rainbow shone no more dazzling than the love in Sarah's face. Both shouted *home.*

Sarah put an arm around each of the children and softly said, "Welcome to the Diamond S. We sometimes call it Rainbow's End. We don't believe in leprechauns, and we don't have pots of gold, but we have far greater treasure here: happiness."

"And no mountain lions?" Timmy prodded, with a big-eyed glance at the corral filled with horses and cowboys.

Seth's blue eyes twinkled. "No mountain lions, but I'm as hungry as one. How about you, buckaroo?"

Timmy nodded and hitched his too-big

pants farther up onto his stomach. His thin face lit up with anticipation. But Ellie continued to watch the rainbow until its glorious colors faded and disappeared before following Seth and Sarah into her new home. . . .

Other memories crowded in on Ellie and demanded her attention, so many she could scarcely contain them. After all the turbulent years with Pa, she and Timmy had found a home that long-ago day. A home and seven years filled with love.

Faces trooped through Ellie's mind like soldiers on parade: Matt, Sarah, and their two boys, Caleb and Gideon. Seth, Dori, and their adorable twin girls, Susannah and Samantha. Curly and Katie Prescott, with their children Riley and Kathleen. A bevy of laughing Mexican children who called Ellie Senorita and giggled when they saw her.

Vaqueros and vineyard workers. People at church in Madera.

Last of all, Solita's smiling face gladdened Ellie's heart. A lump parked in the girl's throat. Solita, *little sun,* healer of bruises and bringer of sunshine to all. How many tears had been shed on the housekeeper's apron? How many times had the wise woman offered comfort without ever speaking a word? The touch of her work-worn hand on Ellie's head soothed away childish hurts like salve on a wound.

Calico nudged Ellie, as if reminding her they needed to head back to the ranch. But Ellie could not go without another prayer of thanks for one of the most important days of her life. Heart overflowing, she slipped from the rock and knelt.

"Lord, thank You so much that Gus allowed Matt and Sarah to adopt Tim and me. Matt never told us how he knew I hated being a Stoddard. Perhaps he guessed." She thought of the seemingly endless time she and Timmy had waited for Matt's return from St. Louis. Before he left, he had told the family, "I don't trust doing this by mail. I'm going to sew Gus Stoddard up so tight that if he ever decides to renege on his bargain, he won't have a legal leg to stand on."

Ellie never asked, but she suspected Matt had paid Gus for her and Timmy. The important thing was they'd been set free. Tears gushed. The first time Matt introduced her as Ellie Sterling, she'd nearly burst with pride. She still did. As the adopted children of one of the richest ranchers in the valley, she and Timmy could "walk tall," as Matt said, and hold their heads high.

Calico shoved her nose against Ellie's shoulder, obviously wanting attention. Ellie patted the mare's neck and obliged. "That's just what I'm going to do when I sing in church tomorrow," she told her faithful horse. "Hold my head high, even though I'm scared out of my wits." Calico whinnied and tossed her mane. "I just hope I don't faint and disgrace the family." Ellie grimaced. "Now where did that horrid thought come from? I've sung in church before." She grimaced. "Just not when a new preacher will be here. Maybe I should tell Matt to get someone else."

God gave me a voice and expects me to use it. Am I going to let the minister of some fancy church keep me from glorifying God with my talent?

Ellie felt a wave of shame crawl up from the bandana around her neck. "No, but I'd better practice." She snatched up her sombrero, jammed it onto her head, and swung into the saddle. A quick touch of her heels to Calico's sides sent the two of them on their way. Ellie opened her mouth and sang the song she had made her own, each note crystal clear:

"When peace, like a river, attendeth my
way,

45

When sorrows like sea billows roll;
Whatever my lot, Thou hast taught me to
    say,
It is well, it is well with my soul."

It is well, echoed back from the wooded hills.

With my soul . . . The echo came again, and Ellie's voice soared in triumph. "It is well, it is well, with my soul!"

Filled with the joy of living, Ellie sang the second and third verses then poured her heart into the final stanza:

"And Lord, haste the day when the faith
    shall be sight,
The clouds be rolled back as a scroll;
The trump shall resound, and the Lord shall
    descend,
Even so, it is well with my soul."

The final note shimmered in the still air. Ellie leaned forward and called in Calico's ear, "Run!" The mare leaped forward. Ellie bent low, exulting in the feel of wind whipping against her face. A glance at the sky showed she had stayed far too long on the promontory. If she didn't get home and into the lovely yellow dress and white mantilla Sarah had bought her, the fiesta would start without the guest of honor!

Ellie reached the ranch house, skidded to a stop by the corral, and dismounted. Then she tossed Calico's reins to one of the hands lounging against the rail. "Take care of her, will you, please?"

He doffed his Stetson and gave her a wide grin. "*Si,* senorita."

A small tornado in a cowboy suit raced toward her. "Hey, Aunt Ellie," Caleb shouted, "where've you been? Folks are comin', and everybody's ready but you. Even Uncle Tim." He pointed toward a group of men standing nearby.

"Oh, dear! If Tim's ready, then I really am late!" Ellie started toward the house at a dead run, then glanced back at the sturdy boy trying to keep up with her. "Thanks, partner." She started to whip around but her momentum carried her forward. She lurched for a few more steps and tried to ignore the muffled laughter she suspected was incited by the spectacle she was providing.

Tim confirmed her suspicions by hollering, "Hey, Ellie, looks like you have two left feet. Don't ask me to square-dance with you!"

She ground her teeth, wanting to throttle her brother. Wasn't it humiliating enough to stagger like a newborn calf or a rowdy cowboy on a Saturday night spree? The last thing she needed was for Tim to call more attention to her plight!

Ellie made a final desperate effort to regain her footing. Just when she thought she'd make it, disaster struck again. One foot slipped. She lost her balance and pitched forward. Her arms flailed but could not stop her from falling. A heartbeat later, she crashed smack-dab into a large, immovable object. Ellie hit so hard she reeled backward.

Strong arms closed around her.

Furious at her clumsiness and even more with Tim, Ellie jerked free. She looked up.

And up.

A stranger towered over her. A stranger wearing a broad grin, whose gray eyes were alight with amusement.

FIVE

Ellie gaped at the man looming over her. Her hands clenched. How dare he look as if he was ready to join in the raucous laughter coming from behind her? She reared back to escape the stranger's amused gaze — and ran head-on into Caleb.

He clutched at her and let out a warning yelp, but it was too late. *Thud.* They landed on the hard ground in an ignominious heap.

"Ow! Get off, Aunt Ellie. You're breaking me!"

Embarrassment gave way to concern. Ellie rolled over and sat up. "I am so sorry," she told her nephew. "Are you hurt?"

"Naw." Caleb scrambled to his feet. He frowned and flexed his arm. "Uh, not bad."

"Let me look." She rolled up his plaid sleeve and inspected his elbow, but after a quick glance, Caleb squirmed and protested.

"Let me go, Ellie. I ain't bleeding. Solita

49

says if you're hurt much, you bleed." He tugged his shirtsleeve back down and grinned at her.

Relief flowed through her. "Thank goodness you're all right."

Caleb gave her a gap-toothed grin and announced with childish candor, "You better get cleaned up. You're a mess." He brushed dust off his shirt and trotted away, leaving her sitting on the ground.

Caleb's comment on Ellie's appearance brought a fresh surge of humiliation, interrupted by a deep voice from which all trace of merriment had fled.

"May I help you?"

Viewed from her lowly position, the tall stranger who blocked the summer sky took on mountainous proportions. The words *you've done quite enough* trembled on Ellie's tongue. She bit them back. The man was in no way to blame for her mowing down Caleb. Ellie wordlessly took the hand he offered, noting its strength in spite of her agitation. "Th–thank you," she stammered.

When she managed to get back on her feet, Tim's laughter-choked voice tightened her lips into a straight line. Ellie freed her hand and whirled, intending to get even with her brother if it was the last thing she did. He forestalled her — and made matters worse.

"You probably haven't been properly introduced, even though I see you've already run into our visiting minister." Mischief danced in Tim's brown eyes. "Reverend Stanhope, meet my sister, Ellie Sterling."

Minister? Reverend? Ellie shut her eyes, wishing the hard-packed earth would open and swallow her.

The stranger laughed. "Make that Pastor. Better yet, Joshua or Josh. I'm not much on formality." A puzzled expression crept into his gray eyes. "Are you the Miss Sterling who will be singing in church tomorrow?"

Ellie couldn't have answered if her life depended on it.

Not so Tim. "Yup." He smirked. "We're all mighty proud of our Ellie's singing."

Why must he babble like the brooks that tumbled down the mountainside to the rivers below? Ellie wondered, wishing her brother were in China or Timbuktu — anywhere far enough from the Diamond S to keep him from adding to her misery.

"Then we'll be in for a treat," Josh said. "What will you be singing, Miss Sterling?"

Her tongue cleaved to the roof of her mouth.

"Call her Ellie," Tim urged, "although

51

folks around here call her the Sierra Songbird."

Ellie had never been more embarrassed. Why did Tim have to brag on her? Now she'd be more nervous than ever, singing in front of the visiting minister. Josh's understanding look helped. His expression plainly showed he knew all about younger brothers. It helped to restore a tiny bit of her dignity.

"I'll settle for 'Miss Ellie,' if that's all right with her," Joshua said.

"Sure it is." Tim patted Ellie's shoulder. "Caleb's right. You're a mess. Get a move on if you're gonna put on some fancy duds before the fiesta starts."

Ellie shot Tim a fiery glance, turned her back on him, and summoned a smile for Josh. "If you'll excuse me, I'll do just that. Oh, I plan to sing 'It Is Well with My Soul.'" She started to pass Josh, but his deep voice stopped her.

"Although that's one of my favorite hymns, would you mind saving it?"

Humiliation engulfed her. "You don't want me to sing tomorrow?"

"Oh, no! I'm looking forward to hearing you," he quickly assured. "It's just that a different song will fit my sermon better. Do you know 'The Ninety and Nine'?"

"Sure she does," Tim blared. He began to

sing. " 'There were ninety and nine . . .' "

A twinkle leaped into Josh's eyes before he said, "Begging your pardon, Tim, but I think we'd best let your sister sing tomorrow."

Tim stuck his nose in the air. "Well! Some folks don't recognize good music when they hear it. I'll save my singing for the horses and cattle. They don't seem to mind when I bed them down for the night." His cheerful grin spoiled his false indignation.

Ellie felt her face scorch. Was there no end to Tim's shenanigans? "I know the song and will be glad to sing it." She climbed the steps to the veranda, snatching at the reins of her temper. A minute more, and she'd be screeching at Tim. But her rage weakened when he said, "Wait till you hear her, Josh. Ellie can beat a western meadowlark all hollow when it comes to singing." Pride rang in every word.

Josh's quick "I'll bet she can" sent tingles through Ellie. She raced inside, through the great hall, and up the broad staircase to her room.

Heedless of her dusty riding skirt and the need to bathe and change clothes, Ellie dropped to her bed. She idly fingered the rich tapestry of the handwoven Mexican spread: red, emerald green, and white —

the national colors of Mexico. Matching draperies hung at the large casement windows set deep into the thick adobe walls.

Ellie only covered the windows while dressing. She loved watching the moon and stars from her bed on nice nights and the rain sluicing down the windowpanes in stormy weather. She thrilled to jagged lightning bolts and even the boom of thunder.

"Well, Lord, I feel like I just came through a thunderstorm," she said. "My nerves are twanging like the strings of my guitar when it's out of tune." She paused. "Joshua Stanhope sure is polite. Outside of Matt and Seth, he seems to be the nicest man I've ever met. I can hardly wait to hear him preach tomorrow." Ellie screwed up her face. "Wish I could say the same for wanting to sing. At least I won't have to face him during my solo. I do not need a reminder of how we met." She felt a reluctant smile curve her lips. "Lord, I know it will be well with my soul, but I'm going to need Your help to settle the rest of me down."

For the first time since she'd crashed into Josh, Ellie had wits enough to remember more than how tall Josh was and the way he'd looked at her. At first, laughter had lurked in his eyes, as if held back by sheer willpower. She'd seen it replaced with compassion. And after Tim prattled on about her singing, genuine interest and admiration flickered in the gray depths. Now Ellie pictured his short, well-brushed light hair and his honest countenance.

"It's like goodness shines through him," she whispered. "Is it because he's a minister?" She shook her head. No. She'd met many ministers — godly men who gave their lives to the service of the Master. Yet never had she seen one whose presence affected her so deeply as Joshua Stanhope had done during their brief encounter. She'd always been too practical to believe in love at first sight, but now she wondered. . . .

A knock brought Ellie out of her reflections. "Are you about ready?" a woman's voice demanded. "May I come in?"

"Of course." Ellie clambered off the bed and opened the door. Sarah stepped inside, lovely in a light blue, tiered fiesta dress that matched her eyes. "Sorry, but I had a little accident and —"

"And landed at a certain handsome stranger's feet," Sarah finished with a trill of laughter.

"You heard?" Ellie's heart sank.

"Everyone heard, thanks to that rascally Tim." Mischief sparkled in Sarah's eyes, and she cocked her head to one side. "Just remember. God brings good from everything that affects His children."

Ellie grunted. "I made a fool of myself in front of a visiting minister, Sarah!"

Sarah donned an innocent expression. She cocked her head to one side and placed her hands on her hips the way Solita did when about to deliver a lecture. She even sounded like Solita when she said, "Land sakes, child. Every single girl, young woman, and eligible widow in Madera will be doing somersaults up and down Main Street to attract Joshua Stanhope's attention if he becomes our minister. Especially Amy Talbot. You have to admit, Ellie, you have a running start." Sarah giggled but didn't look at all repentant. "Sorry. You probably don't care for the word *running* right now."

Ellie laughed in spite of herself, but annoyance swept through her at thought of the petite and predatory Amy, with her oh-so-perfect blond curls and fluttering eyelashes.

"You're right. *Running* isn't my favorite word at the moment. As for Amy being a minister's wife . . ."

"My sentiments exactly." Sarah's eyes twinkled. "So how about getting you into your fiesta dress so you can do something to help prevent such a catastrophe?"

Ellie felt as if she'd been struck. She sank back down on her bed. "I can't. I'm no more fit to be a minister's wife than Amy is."

"Why not?" Sarah sounded genuinely astonished. "You aren't still holding on to the past, are you?" She sat down next to Ellie. Sympathy filled her face.

Ellie twisted her hands. How could she confess that the little girl who cowered before Gus Stoddard still lurked inside, coloring her attitude toward love and marriage? It wasn't right to open old wounds by reminding Sarah that she'd once felt unworthy to marry Matt. The subject had remained closed ever since they talked about it years earlier, at the time of Ellie and Tim's adoption. Yet in spite of all the love that surrounded Ellie, childhood scars had not completely healed over. She hadn't realized how raw they still were until Sarah teased her.

Don't be a ninny, Ellie told herself. *Joshua Stanhope would never fall in love with me. Even if he did, marrying me would be asking for trouble. Minister's wives have to be beyond reproach, not related to the likes of Gus Stoddard. Josh would find himself out of a job and eventually begin to hate me.*

Sarah clasped Ellie's hands in hers. Warm tears cascaded. "Ellie, honey, you are my sister. You are also Matt's and my beloved daughter, but much more. The apostle Paul tells us that when we accept Christ, old things are passed away. All things become new, including us." She dropped Ellie's hands and gathered her into a close embrace. "You are a Sterling, Ellie, not a Stoddard. Don't look back." She gave a shaky laugh. "Remember what happened to Lot's wife. You don't want your partners at the fiesta lugging around a pillar of salt, do you?"

"No." Ellie hugged Sarah, warmed by the fragile feeling that just maybe things would be all right, after all. "Thank you."

Tim's bellow from beneath the window broke into the tender moment. "Hey, Ellie, are you coming or not?"

Caleb's shrill, "Yeah, Aunt Ellie. Where are you?"

Sarah wiped away her tears. "So much for private conversations on your birthday." She ran to the window. "Hold your horses, you two. It's Ellie's birthday. She'll come when she's ready." She turned from the window, hurried to the large wardrobe, and took out Ellie's fiesta dress. Each tier of the sunshiny yellow skirt and modest, ruffled neckline wore bands of white lace that matched the mantilla Sarah laid on the bed. "Are you going to be all right?"

For now trembled on Ellie's lips but she quickly substituted, "Yes." She summoned a smile. "Better get down there before they send out a search party."

"Yes, ma'am!" Sarah saluted. But before leaving the room, she looked straight into Ellie's eyes. "Remember what Matt tells us. 'Walk tall and hold your head high.' You have every right: You are God's child — and ours." The door closed behind her, leaving Ellie feeling as if she'd been sitting in the sunlight for a very long time. She hurried through a sponge bath and slipped into the lovely gown. Her fingers shook as she stepped to the mirror and pinned the mantilla on her dark brown hair.

Pleased with the reflection that stared back at her, Ellie muttered, "First impressions may be lasting, but here's hoping the way I look now will erase Joshua Stanhope's memory of me sprawled at his feet." She snatched up a stiff, white-lace fan, swept out of her bedroom, down the staircase, and into the swirl of the fiesta.

Six

Buggies and buckboards. Carriages and cowboys. Would they never stop arriving? Ellie stood on the veranda, tingling with excitement. Half the countryside must have come to honor her on her birthday. The sound of jingling spurs whipped her around. She stared at Tim. "What are you doing in those clothes?"

Tim smirked. "You like, *mi hermana*?" He smoothed down the short, black jacket lavishly embroidered in silver and ran his hands down the tight, black pants bound at the waist by a scarlet sash. *"Soy un gran caballero."*

Ellie fixed her fascinated gaze on the widest Mexican sombrero she'd ever seen. "There's enough silver braid and conchas on that hat to give you a headache. What are you going to do? Fight a cow or do the Mexican hat dance?"

Tim put on a wise look and stroked his

fake mustache. Ellie suspected one of the horses in the corral had a bald spot. "I might." He glanced over his sister's shoulder and into the yard. His voice dropped to a whisper. "Hey, take a gander at Red Fallon over there with our new minister. Red looks prouder than a mama cow with a new calf."

Ellie surveyed the tall cowboy whose red hair showed streaks of silver. "He does, but Joshua Stanhope isn't our minister yet."

"He will be if *she* has anything to say about it," Tim drawled. He nodded toward a pink-clad girl and her father approaching Red and the minister. She wore an unmistakable where-have-you-been-all-my-life expression. "Amy Talbot has her daddy wrapped around her little finger, and Luther's chairman of the church board. C'mon. We'll go rescue Josh."

"We? I don't think so." Ellie put her fan up to smother a giggle and watched Josh free his arm from the white hand Amy had laid on it. "Besides, he looks perfectly capable of taking care of himself."

"He's probably used to women on his trail," Tim agreed. "But Amy's after anyone wearing pants. She even flirts with me."

"You should feel honored," Ellie teased. Satisfaction at being able to get even with her brother erupted into another giggle.

61

"After all, she's an older woman, and —"

Tim snorted. "Yeah. Just like you. You're pretty near an old maid, you know!" He settled the gigantic sombrero more fully and marched down the veranda steps, spurs clanking. A few long strides took him to the foursome they'd been discussing. Tim said something to Josh and glanced in Ellie's direction. The minister promptly left the others and headed toward the veranda.

Ellie's breath caught when she observed Amy's pout and the scowl on Luther Talbot's face. If Joshua Stanhope wanted to become minister of Christ the Way Church in Madera, walking away from the Talbots was not a good way to secure the position. Josh reached the bottom step. The desire to warn and protect him caused Ellie to say in a low voice, "The Talbots don't look happy about your leaving them."

Mischief shone in Josh's gray eyes, but all he said was, "They don't, do they?" Then he added, "Your brother suggested I go over the order of service with you for tomorrow. No one should object to that, should they?"

The feeling of being in cahoots with him against a common enemy made laughter bubble up past Ellie's ruffles. "They shouldn't." The words *it doesn't mean they won't* hung unspoken in the air.

"I know I'm a stranger, but would you consider allowing me to escort you for at least part of the fiesta?" Josh looked back at the Talbots. "Perhaps you can alert me to any . . . uh . . . pitfalls that lie ahead, should I be accepted as your minister."

Ellie's spirits rose, lighter than the balloons decorating the yard. Brighter than the dozens of luminaries to be lit at dusk. Not trusting herself to speak, she smiled and nodded. She felt a blush begin at the modest neckline of her gown. As it worked its way up, Ellie took refuge behind her fan. She held it so only her eyes showed, praying they wouldn't give away the unexpected feelings churning inside her.

Josh didn't seem to notice her confusion. "Shall we go over the service so we can join the fiesta?"

Ellie sternly bade her unruly heart to be still. She might never see Josh again after tomorrow. So why should she feel he might be the long-awaited stranger she'd yearned for each time she saw Matt and Sarah's happiness? Or the way Seth and Dori shared understanding glances? Or the teasing between Curly and Katie?

The notion left her breathless. But as the fiesta continued, her sense of wonder increased: bittersweet and haunting, like a persistent cloud dimming the sunshine of Ellie's day. Amy Talbot's obvious but futile attempts to pry Josh away from Ellie's side didn't help. Or the bevy of girls and young women who flocked around them, waiting to be introduced and expressing delight at Josh's coming.

When Josh turned away to greet a newcomer, Tim sidled up to his sister. "I gotta hand it to you, Ellie." Admiration filled his voice. "Our new minister's a goner. You've got him roped, tied, and liking it."

"What?" Ellie croaked, feeling the telltale red creeping into her face again. "Josh is just being polite."

"Horse feathers!" was Tim's inelegant reply. "Just watch your step. Amy's wearing her hunting expression and loaded for bear. And she isn't the only one."

Ellie couldn't help laughing, but Tim's remark made her recall Sarah's prediction: *"Every single girl, young woman, and eligible widow in Madera will be doing somersaults up and down Main Street to attract Joshua Stanhope. . . . You have to admit, Ellie, you have a running start."* Ellie bit her lip. She must not let the young minister's marked attentions go to her head.

Event followed event. Josh remained at Ellie's side, except when participating in the games and races. If his broad smile was an accurate indication, he was having the time of his life. He joined in the three-legged race with Tim, so awkward they thumped to the ground after only a few steps and earned the good-natured jeers of the onlookers. At Tim's insistence, Josh accepted the loan of a Diamond S gelding and entered the horse race. He rode well but was no match for his range-trained opponents. He came in last.

A little later, a score of men and boys lined up for a foot race. Josh sprang forward at the starting gun, widened the gap between him and his competitors, and outdistanced them all. He accepted the blue ribbon but said, "Put the cash prize in the collection plate tomorrow. The church needs it more than I do." It earned him a loud cheer of approval from the merrymakers.

When Josh returned to Ellie, his mouth twitched. "Did I redeem myself?"

"Of course. Where'd you learn to run like that?"

"I was talking about the three-legged race, not the foot race." The twitch grew more pronounced.

Ellie felt her mouth fall open. She tried three times before she could speak. "You — you — are you saying you fell down on purpose?" she stuttered.

A mysterious light came into his eyes. "Shhh! Don't tell Tim, but I thought if folks saw me sprawled on the ground, maybe they'd forget your spill."

Ellie's heart lurched. What kind of person was Josh? They'd just met, yet he'd cared enough about her feelings to turn attention from her clumsiness to his. "You redeemed yourself. Thank you." Ellie could say no more.

A fiesta highlight was the piñata hung on a tree branch. One by one, Matt and Sarah blindfolded the children and gave them a long pole. Each had three chances to strike and break the burro-shaped container and set the children scrambling when candy and toys showered down. Yet child after child struck and missed, or only rocked the piñata.

At last the time came for Curly and Katie's children to try. They looked wide-eyed up at the piñata. Riley's lip quivered. "It's too high."

"We're too little," Kathleen said. Tears sprang to her Irish blue eyes.

Ellie wanted to cry, too. Why hadn't they hung a piñata on a lower branch to give the smaller children a chance? Evidently this one was stronger than most. Neither of the Prescotts would be able to break it if the bigger kids hadn't succeeded.

Quick as a flash, Josh demanded, "Where are those poles? No blindfolds for us. We'll show you how to break a piñata." He scooped Riley up in one arm and Kathleen with the other. Then he snatched a pole from Tim and said, "Kids, put your hands above mine. Everyone else stand back."

The crowd fell silent and edged away.

"Ready. Set. Swing!"

Crack. The pole smashed into the piñata. It burst and spilled its contents onto the ground below. A great shout went up from the crowd. The children surged forward. Tim restrained the others while Josh lowered the Prescotts. "Riley and Kathleen get a head start," Tim said. "They broke the piñata."

Moments later, happy laughter rang across the yard — but none happier than Ellie's. If Josh hadn't already redeemed himself, his caring actions with the disappointed little ones would have done the trick. Needing time to sort out her turbulent feelings, Ellie slipped away to her room. She crossed to the window and stood so she could remain unobserved but view the throng stretching from yard to corral and beyond.

A parade of children — led by Caleb and his brother Gideon — crowded close to

Josh, holding up their treasures for him to see. Their delighted shouts curved Ellie's lips in a sympathetic smile. She thought of Jesus. He, too, had gathered the children around Him. He had ordered His disciples not to turn them away, as Luther Talbot was vainly attempting to do with the children below. What a wonderful, godly father Josh would make!

Ellie left the window and removed her lace mantilla. Lovely as it was, she longed for the cool evening breeze to waft through her hair. Besides, this was no time to think about Joshua Stanhope's qualifications for fatherhood. Not with the fiesta reaching its height. Not when the spicy aroma of barbecued beef drifted up to tantalize and remind her of the long plank tables resting on sawhorses and laden with food. Not when several fiddlers and the best square dance caller in Madera county waited to step into the limelight and provide joy for young and old alike.

Ellie felt her face flame with anticipation. She loved square dancing and never lacked for partners, especially freckle-faced Johnny Foster, who used to deliver telegrams to the Diamond S. For the past year or two, his worshipful gaze followed Ellie whenever she encountered him.

She washed her hands, cooled her sun-warmed face, and whispered, "Will Joshua dance with me? Or does he refrain from dancing because of his calling?"

There was but one way to find out. With a last, reassuring glance in the mirror, Ellie left her bedroom. At the top of the staircase, she checked to make sure she was alone. Then she bundled her skirts around her, slid down the banister rail, and hurried back to the fiesta — and Joshua Stanhope.

SEVEN

Joshua watched Ellie Sterling vanish inside the heavy front door of the Diamond S ranch house. A pang went through him, as if with her going he'd lost something precious. He scoffed at the idea. In his years as minister of Bayview Christian he'd been flattered and fawned on, praised and put upon. He'd been pursued by marriage-minded maidens who made it clear they considered him the answer to their own and their scheming mothers' prayers. Yet his heart had kept its steady rhythm in spite of their wiles — and in spite of his mother forever producing suitable candidates for his affections.

Josh smothered a grin. Avoiding the little traps set for him had grown to be a game. He'd secretly enjoyed foiling the elaborate plans laid to ambush him. The last thing he wanted — then or now — was some female hot on his trail. Josh pictured Beryl West-

70

field's lips curled with scorn. After Edward finished flitting from woman to woman and asked the dark-haired woman to marry him, Beryl had delighted in goading Josh. Disgusted with her prodding, Josh once asked, "Whatever happened to modest maidens who allowed the men to do the pursuing?"

Beryl had hooted. "That idea went out with hoopskirts, Josh. Women have as much right as men to go after what they want."

A small hand slipped beneath Josh's arm and brought him back to the present. He looked down into Amy Talbot's upturned face. The avid gleam he'd learned meant another hound on his trail sparkled in the girl's eyes. Josh choked back annoyance. Good thing the tiny blond couldn't read his mind. Red Fallon had already stated how much influence she had with her father — and that Luther ran the church board as if the other members had been hired to do his bidding.

"Reverend Stanhope, will you lead the Virginia Reel with me?" Her confident expression showed she believed her invitation was the same as accepted.

Josh inwardly sighed and freed himself. "Thank you, Miss Talbot, but I don't dance."

A pout replaced her smile. "Oh, but you

must," she gushed. "Why, everyone in Madera dances." She batted her golden eyelashes at him and moved closer. The scent of heavy perfume assailed Josh's nostrils. "If you don't know how, I'll teach you."

"Thank you for your kindness, but I must decline. I really don't care to learn."

A loud *harrumph* sounded from behind them. Josh turned on his heel, expecting to see a scowling Luther Talbot. Instead, the tall, gaunt man wore what Josh figured was as near a look of approval as he could muster.

Luther harrumphed again. "Commendable, Reverend Stanhope. Very commendable. Run along now, Amy. I want to speak with the reverend about tomorrow's sermon." He gave a glance of disapproval toward the merry crowd choosing partners for the square dancing. "We'll just step off a ways to where we can hear ourselves think."

Dismay shot through Josh. Good grief, was this officious-acting man going to tell him what to preach and how?

Luther hooked a bony finger in his vest. "What text are you using?"

Josh didn't like Luther's waiting-to-pass-judgment look. "Matthew 18. The lost sheep."

"Hmmm." Luther's nostrils quivered as if

warding off a bad smell. "Not wise. Not wise at all. This is primarily cattle country, you know." He sniffed. "Although a few . . . uh . . . sheepherders do come to church."

A lesser man would have quailed at the scornful look that accompanied the criticism, but Josh kept his voice steady, although apprehension stirred within him. "That's why I chose the story," he said. He almost added *sir,* but discarded it. If he were to become pastor of Christ the Way Church, he didn't intend to kowtow to a local dictator. Josh had dealt with them before. The only way to handle such men was to show strength.

Luther Talbot's eyebrows threatened to shoot off the top of his head. "I beg your pardon?"

First round. Stanhope, 1. Talbot, 0. The irreverent thought exploded into a hearty laugh. "The story shows God's boundless love for those who have wandered away. Red says the church will be packed tomorrow. Cowboys will be riding in from the ranches to 'check out the city preacher.' Maybe even a few extra sheepherders." Josh's heart bumped against his chest wall. "I pray some of them will be touched enough to want to return."

Luther snorted. "The only reason they'll

come to church is because Dunlap's saloon is closed on Sunday."

Josh fought a wave of hostility for the self-righteous man but contented himself with saying, "Thank God for that." No sense antagonizing the chairman any sooner than absolutely necessary.

Luther shrugged. "What we want in a minister is someone who will tend to the flock, not spend time consorting with range riffraff."

Rage licked at Josh's veins. Was this how Jesus had felt when He cleared the temple of money changers? The young minister set his jaw, longing to shake the hypocrite who dared dictate to him. Josh clenched his teeth. If this was a sample of what he'd have to endure in Madera, the best thing would be to preach in the morning as promised, then catch the first train back to San Francisco.

We need you. Bad.

Memory of Red's cry for help echoed in Josh's ears, followed by a vision of Ellie Sterling's crystal blue eyes looking up at him. He felt his anger die. With it went uncertainty about the future. His heart leaped like an antelope. He would not turn tail and run. If given the chance, he'd accept the challenge of pastoring Christ the

Way Church — and trust in the Lord for the wisdom to handle the battles that surely lay ahead.

In the meantime, Luther was waiting for him to respond.

Josh looked straight into his opponent's unfriendly eyes. "Jesus tells us in Luke 5:32 that He came not to call the righteous, but sinners to repentance."

A heavy hand fell on Josh's shoulder. "A good thing for me," Red's voice boomed. "I wouldn't be here now 'cept for that."

Luther gave an unpleasant laugh. "That may be, but it's the righteous who fill the offering plates with money to pay the preacher." Head held high, Luther turned on his heel and marched off.

Second round. Talbot, 1. Stanhope, 0.

"Well, of all the . . . ," Red sputtered. "Don't pay that old windbag any mind. Luther thinks God can't get along without his help, which I say's more like meddlin'." A crooked grin appeared. "Talbot ain't righteous, and he sure don't do much plate fillin'. Makes a big show of how much he puts in, but I happen to know it's nothing compared with what a lot of folks give. Some that can't really spare it."

"How do you know that?" Josh inquired.

Red guffawed. "Word gets 'round when

there's only a few hundred people in town. Hey, looks like folks are gettin' tuckered. Maybe we can talk Miss Ellie into singin' for us."

Alas for Red's hopes and Josh's fervent wish for the girl who had so impressed him to favor them with a song. When approached, she said, "I'll save my voice for church. Besides, Tim's going to do the Mexican hat dance." Her eyes twinkled. "Perhaps you gentlemen would like to join him?"

"Not me," Red said. "I'll leave that to the reverend."

Josh shook his head. "Sorry. There are some here who'd think it was undignified for a minister." He cast a pointed glance at Luther Talbot, who stood nearby, arms crossed and wearing a disapproving look.

A look of understanding crept into Ellie's lovely eyes. How changeable they were! Josh had seen them flash with indignation, soften with concern for Caleb, and surreptitiously observe him.

A burst of music from the Spanish guitars that had replaced the fiddling filled the air. Josh experienced a multitude of sensations. Had he been unconsciously looking for a mate all the years he avoided entrapment? Had God led him to Madera to find love as

76

well as to preach the gospel? A Bible verse Josh had used while performing weddings sang in his mind: *"For this cause shall a man leave father and mother, and shall cleave to his wife."*

Joy became despair. If Ellie proved to be the wife Josh now realized he'd longed for, it meant further estrangement from his family. The fact she was the daughter of the richest rancher in the San Joaquin Valley wouldn't make her worthy of a Stanhope in the eyes of San Francisco society.

Who cares? Josh fiercely asked himself. *I will not allow Mother or Edward to decide whom I shall marry, only God.*

Relief at having chosen his pathway for better or for worse made Josh feel pounds lighter. He smiled at Ellie. "I can hardly wait to see Tim."

Her eyes darkened. "I just hope he doesn't make a fool of himself. He's only persisting in this because I teased him earlier."

"I wouldn't worry about it." Josh chortled. "I suspect your brother can do anything he sets his mind to."

"I guess we'll find out."

Ellie's concern proved groundless. Tim threw his silver-laden sombrero on the ground, nodded to the musicians, and began his dance. He stomped. He minced with fingers outstretched like a haughty senorita. He circled and leaped. Then amid wild applause and ear-splitting whistles, Tim snatched up the sombrero and swept it to the ground with a low bow. The performance was the funniest thing Josh had seen in years, and it signaled the end of the fiesta.

When the final shouts of, "See you at church tomorrow!" floated back from the multitude of guests, Josh climbed into the backseat of the Fallons' carriage and put his arms around David and Jonathan.

"What hymns would you like tomorrow?" Abby asked. "I'm the organist." By the time they finished their discussion, the boys had fallen asleep. Red and Abby talked in low tones. It gave Josh a chance to relive the hours since Red had met him at the train station and taken him to the Yosemite Hotel.

"It's a ten-mile ride out to the Diamond S. You may wanta change clothes," Red had advised. "A fiesta's no place for city duds." The suggestion proved wise. Once they reached the ranch, Josh had wondered if they'd ever get the dust brushed off.

The day's highlights paraded through Josh's mind, always ending with thoughts of Ellie. Did the little Sierra Songbird really have a voice to rival the western meadowlark? Or did Tim's love for his sister color the boy's judgment? Josh yawned. It had been a long day. Tomorrow would tell . . . and in all probability settle his future concerning Madera and Christ the Way Church.

EIGHT

Even though most of Madera lay quiet and sleeping when Josh returned from the fiesta, he decided to visit the church. His first glimpse of the brown wood building sheltered by trees and topped with a steeple filled him with awe. Light from a full moon and countless stars streamed down like a heavenly benediction. Modest and unassuming, Christ the Way Church could never compete with Bayview Christian. Yet something about it drew Josh.

He stepped inside. Moonlight streamed through the clear glass panes. It lit some of the wooden pews and left others in shadow. He walked up the center aisle and knelt before the altar. Peace fell over him like a mantle.

After a long time, Josh rose and silently slipped out into the glorious night. A sense of Someone walking beside him grew as he began his walk back to the Yosemite Hotel.

"Why does this cow town church cry out to me?" he whispered. No answer came, but the Presence remained. The faith that had led Josh to test God by coming to Madera became knowledge: This was where he belonged.

The next morning, Josh awakened to the chime of church bells summoning the faithful to worship. He sprang from bed and peered out the open window. No fog or shining bay greeted him, only smiling skies and a dusty street leading to Christ the Way Church. Josh filled his lungs with morning air. "Thank You, Lord, for bringing me to this place. Help me speak words of truth and of You."

After a hearty breakfast in the hotel's pleasant dining room, Josh escaped Captain Perry Mace, the talkative proprietor, and hurried to the church. To his delight, the church had lost none of its charm in daylight. The sensation of being inexorably drawn to it intensified, and the sound of music lured him inside. Dark-haired Abby Fallon sat at a small organ. She smiled, continued softly playing, and said, "Good morning. Did you sleep well?"

"Thank you, yes. I'll just put my Bible on the pulpit and get back outside."

Abby's eyes twinkled. "Good idea. Folks

will want to see you."

Josh grimaced. "I know. Preacher on trial and all that." To his amazement, Abby didn't argue. It gave him food for thought.

Josh stepped outside and watched an assortment of conveyances roll up and disgorge their passengers. He saw townspeople, singly and in groups, hurrying up Main Street. Riders hitched their horses to a nearby rail and tried to rid their boots of clinging yellow dust. A battery of eyes turned toward Josh: friendly and welcoming except for the four men who stood with Luther Talbot, all wearing wait-and-see expressions. Josh targeted them as the church board. Luther looked like he'd been drinking vinegar. Had he already expressed doubts about the visiting minister?

"Morning, Josh." A cheerful voice sang out.

He turned to see a grinning Tim Sterling helping Ellie out of a buggy. She looked absolutely fetching in a simple, light-blue gown and matching hat. Josh searched for something to say to keep from betraying his excitement at seeing her again. "Good morning to you both. Nice clothes, Tim. Not as flashy as what you wore for the fiesta, though."

Tim twitched the string tie adorning his

plaid shirt. "Naw. I gave them back to Juan." He cocked his head and blurted out, "How come you're wearing a suit?"

"Tim!" Ellie protested. "That's rude." Color stained her smooth cheeks.

"Why?" her brother wanted to know. "Matt said city preachers mostly wear fancy robes and turn their collars backward."

Josh couldn't stifle his amusement. "Not this preacher. Besides, I may be a country preacher pretty soon."

Tim's enthusiastic *"Yippee-ki-ay"* turned heads and made Josh cringe. But the light in Ellie's eyes and her barely audible "I hope so" helped restore his equilibrium enough to change the subject.

"I forgot to ask Red how the church got its name. It's certainly unusual."

"A real jim-dandy," Tim announced. "Matt and Dori's folks helped build the church. Folks didn't know what to call it, but William Sterling said flat out it was Christ's church and should be named for Him. It's been Christ the Way ever since."

"A good name and a good story," Josh approved.

The church bell pealed a warning note. Tim looked worried. "You better get a move on, Josh. Luther Talbot looks sour enough to curdle milk. C'mon, Ellie." He hurried her up the steps and inside with Josh at their heels.

This is it, Lord, Josh prayed. He took his place on the raised platform. Luther settled into a chair beside him. Josh surveyed the packed church. Sunlight streamed through the clear glass windows. It reflected on steel-rimmed spectacles and Sheriff Meade's badge and sent rainbows dancing around the room. It touched worn hymnbooks and the faces of a congregation far different from Bayview Christian. Clothing ranged from spotless but unfashionable to brand-spanking-new. Captain Perry Mace removed his ever-present top hat and gave Josh an encouraging smile.

Josh's gaze landed on Caleb Sterling. Face still damp from a recent scrubbing, cowlick slicked down, the small boy gave Josh a gap-toothed grin.

It changed the course of the service.

Lord, everyone here needs to hear of Your great love, but none more than the children. Give me the courage to do what I feel I must.

Luther stepped forward, exuding importance. He cleared his throat. "Most of you know that as chairman of the church board, I've been in charge of the services since our former minister moved on to new pastures."

Josh fought the insane desire to howl. *New*

pastures. Bad choice of words. After today's sermon, Luther would be more careful how he used that phrase!

Luther continued. "Reverend Joshua Stanhope is here with us today. I ask for him your kind attention. But first we will sing 'Bringing in the Sheaves.' " He added, "Our Lord told us the harvest is white but the workers are few. This has never been more true than now." Luther droned on and on, louder and more emphatic, until Josh wondered if there would be time for a second sermon.

Luther didn't stop expounding until Tim gave a loud cough and muttered, "Sorry." The chairman nodded at Abby and said, "Let's stand for the opening song."

Josh didn't dare look at Tim. He concentrated on the hymn. Bayview Christian never sang it, but "Bringing in the Sheaves" had been one of Uncle Marvin's favorite songs at the rescue mission. It brought back memories. The down-and-outers had sung it as fervently as this congregation, now on the last line of the refrain: "We shall come rejoicing, bringing in the sheaves."

God, grant that the harvest may be great, Josh prayed.

The song ended. Luther offered a long prayer before directing the congregation to be seated. He returned to his chair and Josh relaxed. Having Luther behind him was a blessing, considering what "Reverend Joshua Stanhope" was going to do.

Blood pounding in his ears until it threatened to deafen him, Josh walked to the front of the platform but didn't step behind the pulpit. "I'm glad to be here with you." He took a deep breath. "Will the children please come forward?"

Eyebrows rose. A gasp from Luther echoed through the church. It did not deter Josh. In all the time he'd been preaching, he'd never been more sure of himself.

At first, no one moved. Josh saw Caleb look at Matt for permission before heading toward the front of the church. Gideon followed; then a whole flock of children surged forward. Josh seated himself on the shallow steps leading up to the platform and motioned for the children to join him. "I have a story for you. Your mothers and fathers are welcome to listen, too."

Luther's chair tipped over with a *bang.* "Really, Reverend, I must protest."

Josh turned. "Please be seated, Mr. Talbot." Their gazes clashed and held. Then to Josh's relief, Luther gave a loud *harrumph* and resumed his place.

Third round. Stanhope, 1. Talbot, 0.

Josh swallowed a chuckle and turned back to the children. "How many of you live on cattle ranches?" he inquired. Several hands shot up.

"How many of you go riding in the hills with your daddies?" Other hands raised.

Josh leaned forward and said in his most mysterious voice, "Do you know that God is a cattle rancher?" He thrilled at the interest in the children's eyes. "God says in the Bible that he owns the cattle upon a thousand hills. I saw a lot of cattle yesterday but not that many!" He kept his attention on the children. "Even though God owns all those cattle, His Son, Jesus, is called the Good Shepherd. That's funny, isn't it?"

The children nodded, but Luther mercifully kept still. Josh went on. "A long time ago Jesus told a story that shows how much God loves everyone. We call it the story of the lost sheep." Josh glanced at the congregation. A small group sitting near the back wore broad smiles; Josh suspected they were the sheep owners. Others in the congregation scowled. Even Tim looked doubtful, but Ellie's blue eyes sparkled.

"A certain man had a hundred sheep. One day when he counted them, one was missing. The man left the other ninety-nine and went to find the sheep that had wandered away from the flock. The story says the shepherd was really happy when he found his sheep and brought it back where it belonged."

"I bet the sheep was happy, too," Caleb piped up.

Josh laughed and rejoiced when the congregation joined in. "I'm sure you're right, Caleb. You may all go back to your parents now." He stood, waited until they scrambled back to their places, then crossed to the pulpit and opened his Bible.

"Isaiah 53:6 says, 'All we like sheep have gone astray; we have turned every one to his own way; and the Lord hath laid on him the iniquity of us all.' " Josh closed his Bible and leaned forward. "You probably wonder why I chose to preach about sheep here in cattle country." He waited for a murmur to die. "I don't know much about cattle and sheep, but I know one important thing: You can herd cattle. Sometimes the ornery critters object and sometimes the herd stampedes, but cattle can still be driven."

Josh leaned forward, aware of quickening interest in the congregation. "Sheep can't be driven. They have to be led by someone who understands them and cares about them. Someone who is willing to give his life to save the flock." He paused. "The biblical account of the lost sheep doesn't list details, but the fact that the shepherd left the ninety and nine in the wilderness shows us the search couldn't have been easy.

"I've asked Miss Sterling to sing a song that tells what the search may have been like. In 1874 a man named Ira Sankey was on an evangelism tour in Scotland with Dwight Moody. Sankey tore a poem from a British newspaper, put it in his pocket, and forgot about it. At a service later that day, Moody asked Sankey for a closing song.

"It caught Ira by surprise, but the Holy Spirit reminded him of the poem. He took it out, said a prayer, and composed the tune as he sang. 'The Ninety and Nine' was Sankey's first attempt at writing a hymn tune." Josh nodded to Ellie. "Miss Sterling." He went back to his chair.

Ellie stepped to the front of the church. Abby played a few notes. Ellie began singing. The first clear note laid a hush over even the smallest child. Josh sat spellbound. Where had this rancher's daughter learned to sing like this? Ellie's voice surpassed the finest soloists who held highly paid positions at Bayview Christian. The words filled the sanctuary:

"There were ninety and nine that safely lay

In the shelter of the fold.
But one was out on the hills away,
Far off from the gates of gold.
Away on the mountains wild and bare.
Away from the tender Shepherd's care."

The song continued, painting unforgettable pictures of the obstacles the shepherd encountered in his quest to find the lost sheep. The congregation sat transfixed. When Ellie reached the final stanza, her voice swelled with joy:

"And the angels echoed around the throne,
'Rejoice, for the Lord brings back His own!
Rejoice, for the Lord brings back His own!' "

Ellie took her seat. Tears crowded behind Josh's eyelids. He rose and slowly walked to the pulpit. He struggled for words to match the triumphant ones lingering in the sunlit air. Finding none, Josh bowed his head and said, "Let us pray."

NINE

When Joshua Stanhope called the children to the front of the church and courteously but firmly squashed Luther Talbot's attempt to interfere, Ellie Sterling wanted to stand up and cheer. Tim's wide grin showed he felt the same way.

The children crowded close to Josh. A sunbeam from the window behind the pulpit bathed the little group with golden light and glorified the young minister's face as he began the story of the lost sheep. Ellie clasped lace-mitted hands and glanced around her. Josh's rich, deep voice and simple retelling of the timeless parable held the congregation spellbound . . . except for Amy Talbot. Face lifted toward Josh, her fingers toyed with the ruffles on her white dress. She coughed behind a dainty handkerchief, then dropped it and made a show of picking it up.

Ellie raged at the disrespectful, obvious

attempt to attract the young minister's attention. Relief surged through her when Josh paid Amy no more heed than if she were a bug on the wall. He finished his story, sent the children back to their parents, and continued with the service.

Ellie drank in every word, finding new meaning in the familiar Bible story. Then Josh nodded to her. She slowly walked to the front of the church. *Lord, let me sing to Your glory.* Abby struck the opening chords. Ellie's earlier apprehension vanished. She opened her mouth and poured her heart into the song. Her heart thrilled at the look of understanding she saw in the faces turned toward her. Cattlemen and sheepmen alike knew every obstacle the Good Shepherd had encountered when He searched for His lost sheep. They, too, battled the elements of an often harsh land. Wild, bare mountains shaken by thunder. Steep and rocky trails and canyons. The desert. Flood-swollen rivers. Starless nights so black they hid dangers that threatened them. Thornbushes that tore into man and beast.

The expressions on the girls' and women's faces reflected their knowledge, as well. In spite of stern warnings, children sometimes wandered away from home. What agony mothers and sisters experienced until they heard the glad cry that showed a child — a lost lamb — had been found.

Never had Ellie felt the effects of a song so strongly. She closed her eyes and sang the final stanza with a power far beyond her own ability:

"There arose a glad cry to the gate of
    Heaven,
'Rejoice! I have found My sheep!'
And the angels echoed around the throne,
'Rejoice, for the Lord brings back His own!
Rejoice, for the Lord brings back His own!' "

The triumphant proclamation lingered in the sunlit air. Ellie returned to her seat, as exhausted as if she'd traveled every foot of the way with the Good Shepherd. Memory of the faces turned toward her and the glistening tear tracks on work-worn faces filled her with humility. Her heart swelled, and she silently thanked God.

Tim patted Ellie's hand, as if aware of her feelings.

Then Josh said, "Let us pray." Heads bowed. "Father, we thank Thee for this day and these, Thy beloved children. May the peace of God, which passeth all understanding, keep their hearts and minds through

93

Christ Jesus. Amen." Josh smiled at the congregation. "Now if you'll give me time to get outside, I'd like to meet you all."

Luther Talbot pushed forward, protest written all over his disapproving face. "Our minister always greets people *inside* the church, not out," he announced.

Josh's easy laugh stretched Ellie's lips into a smile. She poked Tim when he showed evidence of wanting to let out *yippee-ki-ay* after Josh replied, "God has given us such a beautiful day, I'm sure He won't mind if we step outside to enjoy it." He strode down the aisle, leaving Luther huffing behind him in hot pursuit, with Amy at their heels.

Before they reached the door, her clear treble floated back. "Oh Reverend, your sermon was *wonderful*! I don't know when I've been so touched." She giggled. "Please forgive me. Father said you don't like being called Reverend, but it doesn't seem fitting to call you Josh. How about Preacher Josh?"

Although Ellie couldn't see Amy's face, she could visualize the fluttering eyelashes and trademark innocence that were the finest weapons in the tiny blond's arsenal of charm. How would Josh respond? The first pang of jealousy Ellie had ever known attacked her. *Don't be foolish,* she told her wildly beating heart. *Josh is nothing to you.*

Is that so? a second voice whispered. *You've cared for him from the moment you met.*

Josh's amused voice broke into Ellie's turbulent thoughts and silenced the nagging voice. "I was called Pastor in San Francisco, but Preacher Josh will do. Now if you'll excuse me, we need to make way for others coming out."

"Bravo!" Tim whispered in Ellie's ear. "The Royal Canadian Mounties may always get their man, but I bet Amy Talbot won't. She seems to have met her match."

Ellie stifled a laugh. Yet as she and Tim followed the crowd surging outside to greet Josh, she wondered why Tim's comment should fill her with glee. Was it Christian to be glad Amy was getting the comeuppance she deserved? Besides, what was Joshua Stanhope to Ellie Sterling, or she to him?

She and Tim reached the doorway and stepped out into the sunshine. Sarah's laughing remark about the female population trying to attract Joshua Stanhope's attention had already come to pass. Girls and women in billowing summer dresses encircled him. High-pitched voices praised the sermon, the story, and Josh.

Don't set your cap for him, Ellie told herself. *Josh showed a clear preference for you at the fiesta, but look at him now.* Sarah's reminder that she had a running start didn't silence Ellie's doubts. She turned her attention to a group near her and concentrated on their comments.

"He's a likely young feller. Lookit the way he put ol' man Talbot in his place."

"Yeah, but he didn't preach much. Just told stories."

"That's the way I like it," someone approved. "Short 'n' sweet. Preachers that rattle on and on usually just keep repeatin' themselves."

"Wonder what the church board will do? Talbot looks mad enough to send Stanhope packin'." A laugh followed.

"I don't take much stock in what the Talbot girl says, but I kinda like the name Preacher Josh. It's friendly sounding."

"Pree-cisely," another drawled. "I figured he might be uppity, being from a big city and all. He ain't a bit like that." The speaker lowered his voice, and Ellie had to strain her ears to hear. "I hear tell his folks live in a swell mansion. Funny he'd leave all that an' some big church to come to Madera."

"Not funny at all," a crisp voice argued. "I wouldn't live in San Francisco if they gave me the place. Madera's good enough for me."

A murmur of agreement rose before the first speaker commented, "I shore vote for this new man. I aim to tell Talbot right now." He broke away and headed for Luther.

"Hey, wait for us!" A general exodus in Luther's direction followed. A moment later, Ellie saw the group of men surround the dour chairman. Her heart skipped a beat when they maneuvered him away from the crowd and under a large oak tree. Ellie couldn't hear what they said, but their jutting chins showed they'd met with strong opposition. What if Luther convinced them Josh wasn't worthy to be hired?

Ellie felt perspiration spring to her forehead. Dread tightened her fingers into fists. She clutched her arms around herself to suppress pain. The thought of never seeing Josh again was unbearable. How could he have staked a claim on her heart in such a short time? She held her breath and watched Matt, Seth, Red Fallon, and the four board members join the group under the tree. Now what?

It felt like an eternity to Ellie before Luther raised his hands with a disgusted look. He walked at a snail's pace toward Josh, dragging his feet all the way. "Reverend Stanhope, it has been decided to hire you, contingent upon —"

Loud cheers erupted, but Luther scowled. "As I was saying, the offer is contingent upon your performing acceptably for the next six months."

For the first time in their acquaintance, Ellie saw Josh's jaw tighten. His gray eyes darkened with anger, and his voice rang. "Mr. Talbot, I will be happy to serve Christ the Way, but I do not perform. Any minister who does isn't worth his calling."

Red Fallon stepped to Josh's side and glared at Luther. "We're hirin' a preacher, Talbot, not an actor. Put that in your pipe and smoke it!"

"Yippee-ki-ay!" Tim bounded over to Josh. "I'm gonna be the first one to shake our new preacher's hand."

The excitement on top of the reaction Ellie had experienced from singing proved too much for her. One hand over her rapidly beating heart, she slipped back into the empty church. She sank into a pew, trying to shut out the look Josh had given her just before she fled. And trying in vain to remember that anyone who walked so close to God could never be yoked with a girl who had never stopped hating her father.

Tim found her there a long time later. "C'mon, Ellie. Matt and Sarah invited Josh to the ranch for dinner. He's going with you in the buggy as soon as the rest of the folks here clear out." Tim sighed and rubbed his stomach. "Hope it's soon. Amy's hanging on 'til the last dog's hung, but I think Luther's about ready to drag her home."

It took a moment for his news to sink in. "Josh? Ride with me? What about you?"

"I already got a horse from the livery stable. Josh has to have a way to get back." Tim flashed a mischievous smile. "Now's your chance, sister dear. He's already interested."

Ellie didn't pretend to misunderstand. "Some chance." She couldn't keep bitterness from her voice. Bitterness and longing. "Can you imagine Gus Stoddard's daughter married to someone like Josh?"

Tim's smile disappeared. "You're Ellie Sterling now, not Ellie Stoddard."

His loyalty brought tears. "What if Gus . . . ?"

Tim patted her hand. "Forget about him, Ellie. He was glad enough to get shut of us. Most likely, we'll never see him again. Peter or Ian either."

"Do you ever think about them?" Ellie turned her hand over and clung to Tim's. It suddenly seemed terribly important to hear his answer.

He shrugged. "Not much. They were mean. All three of them."

"Do you hate them?"

"Naw." Tim's brown eyes took on a poignant light. "I used to, but Seth says we gotta love God more than we hate people. We gotta forgive them, too, even when it ain't easy." His sigh sounded like it came up from the toes of his boots.

"If only I could find a way to be worthy of someone like Josh," Ellie whispered.

Tim cleared his throat and gave her fingers a squeeze. "You already are."

"Just ride close to the buggy," she pleaded.

"Sure. Can't let you and our new preacher go buggy riding without a chaperone."

Ellie smiled. Tim had returned to his usual impish self, but she'd caught a glimpse of the man he was well on his way to becoming.

To Ellie's dismay, Luther and Amy still had Josh buttonholed, even though the others had gone. Josh finally said to the Talbots, "If you'll excuse me, it's quite a ride out to the Diamond S, and they're waiting dinner for us. Miss Sterling, are you ready to go?" He nodded toward the buggy.

"You don't mean to say you and Ellie are riding ten miles unchaperoned!" Luther burst out. Disapproval oozed from every word, and Amy's smile changed to a pout.

Tim drew himself up into a picture of outrage. "Of course not. It wouldn't be proper." He pointed to a saddled horse. "I'll be riding alongside the buggy. We'd best be going. Solita doesn't like us to be late for meals."

"*Harrumph.* We will continue our conversation at another time, Reverend. Come, Amy." Luther strode off, but Amy sent a venomous glance toward Ellie before she tripped away and called, "Remember, Preacher Josh. You're to have dinner with us next Sunday."

Ellie could barely control herself at the look on Josh's face. It clearly said he did not enjoy the prospect of dinner at the Talbots.

He helped her into the buggy and asked, "Shall I drive?"

"Please." Self-conscious, she wondered what to say next. She needn't have worried. Josh began to ask about the country, the people, and Christ the Way Church. The trip to the Diamond S had never seemed shorter. By the time they arrived, Ellie knew Tim was right. Incredible as it seemed, "Preacher Josh" was definitely interested in her.

TEN

Ellie had always scoffed at old wives' tales and oft-quoted sayings. When one came true, she chalked it up to coincidence. Yet a week after her discussion with Tim about their father and brothers, something happened that shook her skepticism. It also brought back memories she wanted to forget.

One evening, Seth came into the huge sitting room where the family had gathered after supper. A fire flamed in the huge fireplace and flickered on the colorful tapestries that brightened the walls. Seth walked over to Sarah and sat down beside her. His grim expression sent an alarm bell clanging in Ellie's mind.

"I'm glad you're all here." He slowly took a crumpled envelope from his pocket and pulled out a folded sheet of paper. "When Curly brought the mail home today, this letter was in it."

Ellie's body tensed. She shivered in spite of the warmth from the fire.

"It's from Gus," Seth said.

Tim sent a startled look at Ellie. "Talk of the devil and his horns appear," he mumbled, so low only she could hear him.

Ellie shushed him and turned her attention back to Seth. She'd seldom seen him as serious as when he told Sarah, "This concerns you as well as me."

She gasped, and her face paled. "What does Gus want?"

Seth's face turned thunder-cloud dark. "The usual. Money."

"So what's Gus whining about this time?" Matt barked.

Tim leaped up from the rug where he'd been sprawled at Ellie's feet. "The usual? This time? Has Gus asked for money before? How come I didn't know about it?"

"Settle down," Seth told him. "There was no need for you or Ellie to know. Matt and I took care of it."

Tim's eyes blazed. "You didn't send him money, did you?" he choked out.

"No. We won't this time either."

"Good." But Tim remained on his feet, fiery-eyed and rigid.

Heartache and shame that they were Gus Stoddard's children tightened Ellie's chest.

Why must they face humiliation again, just when she was trying to follow Tim's lead and forgive her shiftless family?

Seth looked even more troubled. "Ellie, I'm sorry you and Tim have to hear this, but you need to know what Gus has to say."

Ellie nodded, unable to get words out of her constricted throat.

Tim snorted. Tall and straight, he flung his head back and said, "I'd rather never hear what he has to say. Is he trying to get Ellie and me back?"

"He can't!" Sarah protested. "Matt made sure of that when we adopted you."

"Gus has ways," Tim reminded her. "Nothing could be worse than our being yanked back to St. Louis."

Amen to that, Ellie silently agreed. "Read the letter, please, Seth."

"All right." He unfolded the page and read:

"Dear Seth,

"I need yer help. Peter and Ian showed up and got in a fight on the docks. A feller died. The boys didn't kill him, but they got tossed in jail anyway. I would of sent a telegram but it takes every penny Agatha and me kin scrape together to get by. It don't seem right, us starvin when you and Sarah are livin in luxury.

"Wire five hundred dollars right away so we kin buy food and bail out yer brothers. You owe me, considering all I done fer you."

Seth threw the letter down. "Five hundred dollars? How dare that miserable excuse for a man come whining to Sarah and me after the way he treated us?"

Ellie cringed, but Tim ground his teeth, snatched up the letter, and read on:

"I can't stand knowin Peter and Ian might git hung. It's bad enough that I give up Timmy and Ellie when I wuzn't thinkin straight. Send the money to . . ."

Tim flung the letter toward the fire, but Ellie sprang from her chair and caught it.

"Why did you do that?" Tim hollered.

She shook her head. "I — I don't know. Something told me it should be saved." Tears dripped on the wrinkled page.

"Aw, Ellie, don't cry. I'm sorry I yelled at you." He looked so contrite that she mopped her eyes and hugged him, glad he didn't jerk away as he usually did when others were present.

Matt came across the room and held out

his hand. "I'm glad Ellie saved it, Tim. Gus's story doesn't ring true. Seth and I will get to the bottom of this. We'll need the letter to investigate."

Ellie handed it to Matt, glad to be rid of the hateful thing. Barren of either *please* or *thank you,* it typified Gus's approach to life: wheedle, whine, and take, take, take. What would Matt discover when he investigated?

Early the next morning, Matt saddled up for the ride to Madera. Seth did the same. And Tim, who flatly refused to stay at the ranch. Matt would send a telegram to the lawyers who drew up the ironclad adoption papers on Ellie and Tim. "It won't take long for them to get the truth about the Stoddards," he said. "I expect an answer before nightfall."

Matt's prediction came true. Late that afternoon, the three horseback investigators returned. Tim leaped from the saddle and onto the veranda where the womenfolk sat waiting. Matt and Seth followed close behind. Tim's grin melted the cold, hard knot crowding Ellie's chest.

"Gus's story has more holes than a tin can used for target practice," he yelled.

"It sure does," Matt put in. "A dockhand who saw the fight cleared Peter and Ian."

The breath Ellie had been holding

106

whooshed from her lungs. Her brothers weren't murderers. Thank God!

Matt continued. "The law released Peter and Ian. They left St. Louis before Gus wrote the letter!"

"That's not all," Tim announced with a look of disgust. "Gus and Agatha don't need food or anything else. Can you beat that? After all his bad luck at gambling, Gus made a killing on the *River Queen.* The lawyer said Agatha grabbed the money and invested it." A look of satisfaction crawled across Tim's excited face. "Serves Gus right."

Seth took up the story. "The lawyer also said that, according to gossip, Agatha only doles out a few dollars at a time to Gus. They have a cottage in a nicer part of town now. The old shack burned shortly after they left."

Good riddance, Ellie thought. She exchanged glances with Tim. His expression showed he shared her relief that the place where they'd endured so much heartache no longer existed.

"I learned a whole lot more from the lawyer." Matt laughed until tears came. "Agatha is the talk of St. Louis. Seems she's bound and determined to make Gus respectable. She descended on every gambling hall he frequented. She brandished an umbrella and threatened dire consequences to anyone who gave him credit. Agatha Stoddard is one determined woman!" Matt wiped his eyes, then sobered.

"I told the lawyer about the letter asking for money under false pretenses. He advised me to put it away for safekeeping. The lawyer is officially warning Gus that if he ever tries any more shenanigans, he'll be jailed for attempted extortion. I seriously doubt we'll be hearing from him again."

A collective sigh of relief went up from the group. Ellie felt a long-carried burden slip away. Was she finally unshackled from the past? A prayer rose from her grateful heart. *Lord, please help Pa. No sheep was ever more lost than he is.*

That night, Ellie lay in bed, watching the stars through her open window. Suddenly the significance of the prayer struck her. For the first time in years, she'd referred to her father as Pa, not Gus. Was it the first step toward forgiveness? She fell asleep pondering the day's events and thanking God for brighter tomorrows.

Joshua Stanhope surveyed his new home and burst into laughter. "Lord, this parsonage could fit in the downstairs of the Nob

Hill mansion with room to spare, but I love it. The church women sure made it shine." He breathed in the resinous smell of furniture polish and the woodsy odor of carpets beaten in the fresh, summer air. Gleaming windows offered an ever-changing parade of swaying tree branches and scolding squirrels. A well-trodden path led between the simple wooden dwelling place and the church.

Josh left his door open to the great outdoors as much as possible. It presented endless ideas for his sermons. He never tired of watching the squirrels and listening to the multitude of songbirds that filled his days with music. They lessened the heartache of the scene with his mother when he went to get his trappings for the move to Madera. Josh never dreamed he'd be hired after his first sermon so had arrived with only limited clothing and none of his personal treasures. Considering his mother's opposition to him leaving San Francisco, it hadn't seemed wise to ask for them to be sent.

The confrontation with her had been intense. So was Josh's parting with Edward. Only Charles Stanhope's firm handclasp and quiet "I'm proud of you for doing what you know you must" eased Josh's regret at causing his mother and brother pain.

He picked up a letter from the hand-hewn table. The words blurred, but he knew his mother's words by heart from many readings:

You will always be my son, Joshua, but I refuse to encourage you in your madness. I spoke to the board at Bayview Christian. They are giving you a six-month leave of absence so that you can come to your senses.

Charles says it isn't legal to withhold the income from your grandfather's trust fund, which I planned to do. However, I warn you: if you continue in your headstrong path, there will be consequences. I implore you to return to San Francisco where you belong. All will be forgiven and never mentioned again.

Your loving mother

Josh put the letter aside, but it had done its work well. For the dozenth time since it arrived, he asked himself, *Is it more than chance for Bayview Christian to approve a six-month leave of absence when my position here is "contingent upon performing acceptably for the next six months"? God, are You giving me a loophole in case things don't work out with Christ the Way after all?*

"No!" Josh slammed his fist on the wooden table so hard it made the bouquet of wildflowers one of the children had brought to his door jump. A sea of faces swam before him: Men, women, children. Old and young. Cattlemen and cowboys. Sheepherders. Townsfolk. Visitors who stayed in Madera before or after taking the scenic stagecoach trip to the Yosemite Valley. "I don't belong in San Francisco," he muttered. "I belong here among those who have welcomed me. And those who haven't. Namely, Luther Talbot."

"Did I hear my name?" a cold voice asked from the doorway.

Josh gritted his teeth and turned. The chairman of the board had a way of popping in like an out-of-control jack-in-the-box, especially on Saturdays. Josh knew from past experience the call would be one of three things: a critique of his latest sermon, a text for the next day, or a complaint about Josh's attempts to carry the gospel outside the church walls. Josh wouldn't stop. In the few short weeks he'd been in Madera, new faces had begun to appear in the congregation, thanks to his and Red Fallon's efforts.

Today's session was a repeat of many others. By the time Luther took his sanctimonious self away, Josh felt like he'd been thrown into a thornbush. Worse, trying to prepare the next day's sermon seemed impossible. How could he concentrate on God with Luther Talbot's presence lingering in the parsonage like a bad smell?

Longing to escape, Josh tramped to the livery stable and saddled Sultan. Matt had given him the black gelding shortly after Josh had returned from his trip to San Francisco.

"You need a good horse. Sultan's strong, smart, and gentle. Treat him well, and you'll have a friend for life," Matt had advised. "If you ever get caught out and don't know your way home, let Sultan have his head. He'll bring you back to the Diamond S."

Now Josh rubbed the gelding's soft nose and swung into the saddle. "You're everything Matt promised and more," he told the superb animal. Sultan stomped one foot and whinnied as if impatient to be off. Josh nudged him into a trot, then a ground-covering canter. Right now the more distance Josh put between himself and cantankerous Luther Talbot, the better.

Eleven

A shadow blocked the late August sunlight streaming through the parsonage doorway. Tim Sterling stepped inside. "Hey, Josh, want to go cat hunting tomorrow?"

Josh stared at his grinning visitor. "Cat hunting! Who hunts cats? I thought they were welcome around here to keep the mouse population down."

Tim rolled his eyes and looked disgusted. "You sure are a city slicker! Not pussycats. Cougars. Mountain lions."

Josh eyed him suspiciously. "Is this another of your jokes?"

Tim shook his head. "Naw." His grin faded. "There've been a couple of cougar sightings. Yesterday, some of our hands combing the draws on the far north side of the range found a downed steer. We're going after the cat that killed it."

"What's a cougar doing on the Diamond S this time of year? I thought they stayed in the mountains until snow came."

Tim scowled. "This one didn't. Maybe he figured he'd get a head start on his buddies. Do you want to go on the hunt or not? Matt says you'll have to stay at the ranch tonight. We leave at daylight."

Josh hid his trepidation at the idea of chasing mountain lions. "Of course I want to go. I'll get Sultan and ride back to the ranch with you."

The next morning, a loud pounding roused Josh from deep sleep. He opened his eyes. How could the window of the parsonage have doubled in size overnight? Who had replaced his gingham curtains with rich, brightly colored draperies?

The pounding resumed, followed by an insistent call. "Get up and grab some grub, or we're leaving without you."

Josh laughed. No wonder he'd been disoriented. The guest room at the Diamond S had little in common with his humble parsonage bedroom. He sprang from bed, tingling with anticipation.

"Be with you in a minute, Tim." He poured water from a pitcher into its matching bowl and splashed his face. "No time to shave. Hope Ellie isn't up," he murmured, then laughed at himself. Living on a ranch meant Ellie had seen lots of unshaven men.

114

He just didn't want to be one of them! His admiration for Ellie had grown by leaps and bounds ever since he'd met her at the fiesta. And each time the Sierra Songbird sang in church, Josh's hopes of some day winning her increased. "If I'm not a goner as Tim says, I'm pretty close to it," he admitted.

"You're slower than molasses in January," Tim accused when Josh followed him down the staircase to the hall and into the enormous kitchen. Josh cast a quick glance around. Good. No Ellie. Just Solita. She beamed and motioned Tim and Josh to the table. She set steaming fried eggs with chili sauce in front of them and a platter of warm tortillas.

"Huevos rancheros."

Josh dove into the egg mixture. "Solita, I don't know anyone in San Francisco who can make these like you do. Delicious."

"*Gracias.*" Her white teeth gleamed in a broad smile. "They stick to the ribs, as Senor Tim says."

"They sure do," Tim said through a mouthful. He gulped down the rest and jumped to his feet when Matt, Seth, and Curly came in. Josh did the same.

The men stepped outside into gray dawn and headed for the corral. But Josh couldn't resist glancing back at the house. An upstairs curtain moved. A girl in a dressing gown appeared at the window, and a soft voice called, "Be careful."

"We will," Tim promised. He vaulted astride the powerful blue roan that stood saddled and waiting. Josh took Sultan's reins from the vaquero who held them and mounted. Matt, Seth, Curly, and several other cowboys swung into their saddles.

Josh chuckled, caught up in the contagion of Tim's excitement. How the Bayview Christian congregation would exclaim if they could see their former pastor now!

"What's funny?" Tim wanted to know. "Settle down, Blue," he ordered his horse.

"I was thinking about my church in San Francisco."

A wary expression crept into Tim's eyes. "You're not going back, are you?"

Josh lowered his voice. "Not unless Luther Talbot convinces folks to kick me out."

Tim shook his head. "He won't do that. Amy won't let him." He hesitated, then said with deadly intensity, "We're pards, right?"

"Of course."

Tim's jaw set. "I gotta warn you. There's talk around town. Amy's bragging she'll be Mrs. Joshua Stanhope before your six months are up." A grin chased away Tim's obvious concern. "Folks are saying she'd better get a move on."

Josh had never been more flabbergasted. "She . . . I . . . what makes her think I'm interested in her?"

"She's Amy. That's enough."

Josh's heart thundered. He bit his tongue to keep from blurting out that Amy would never be Mrs. Joshua Stanhope. The first moment he'd looked into Ellie Sterling's shy blue eyes, the title had been hers for the taking.

Tim waggled his eyebrows. "Don't forget. Cougars aren't the only cats around here." He bent low over Blue's neck and raced off, but soon returned. "Have you ever seen a mountain lion?"

Josh shoved aside the troublesome thought of Amy stalking him. "Hardly. They don't come to Nob Hill."

"I guess not." Tim pulled Blue closer to Sultan. "When Ellie and I first came out here, I was only eight years old and scared to death. Gus told us if we weren't good, the mountain lions would eat us."

"Who is Gus?"

Tim looked surprised. "Gus Stoddard. Ellie's and my pa. Didn't you know? I figured ol' man Talbot would've told you before now."

Josh shook his head. "I thought you were

Sterlings."

Tim's eyes flashed. "We are. Gus sold us to Matt and Sarah a long time ago. Hey, don't tell Ellie I spilled the beans. She hates being reminded we used to be Stoddards." His face brightened. "We don't have to worry about it any longer. Matt got a lawyer to fix it so Gus can't bother us again without being in big trouble."

Good for Matt. From the sketchy information Tim had given, it appeared Gus Stoddard wasn't fit to wipe his children's feet.

Tim didn't seem to notice Josh's silence. He chattered on. "Guess what, Josh? The first mountain lion I saw looked like a sleepy, overgrown pussycat. Seth and I went camping in the mountains about four years ago. A dandy place. Good fishing holes. We were having a great time, but on the way back down the creek to our camp, we heard screaming. It sounded like a woman crying for help."

The look in Tim's eyes sent chills skittering up Josh's spine. "What did you do?"

"Seth said it had to be a mountain lion. They're cowards and don't usually attack folks unless they're cornered — or unless it's a mama cat with cubs. But I was glad Seth had his rifle." Tim grimaced. "Like a dummy, I'd left mine in camp.

"Anyway, Seth had already warned me never to run if I met a cougar and didn't have a gun. It's the worst thing you can do. You need to spread your arms out like an eagle's wings, make yourself look as big as you can, and yell like an Indian on the warpath. And pray hard!"

Josh gripped the reins tighter. "So what happened?"

"We came around a bend in the trail." Tim's eyes glazed over. "There he was, long and yellowish and not mean-looking at all . . . until he opened his mouth." Tim gulped. "That cougar had one sharp set of teeth." A red tide flowed into Tim's face. "I forgot everything Seth said and started to run. He shoved me so hard I hit the ground. He bellowed and threw his rifle to his shoulder, but the cougar leaped into the bushes just before Seth pulled the trigger. The shot missed him."

"Did you track him?"

"Naw. Seth said to let him go." Tim looked shamefaced. "I gotta admit I was glad. Hey, you look kinda pale."

"What do you expect?" Josh retorted. "After hearing your story, I'd just as soon keep my distance from any mountain lions."

"Do you want to go back to the ranch house? Or town?"

"Not on your life. If we see a cougar, you can do your eagle act and protect me."

Tim whooped, but Josh caught his look of relief when he set Blue to dancing across the range. Although Josh's heart persisted in turning somersaults, he realized he'd just passed an important test.

Dusk fell with no sign of mountain lions. The hunting party set up camp a short distance upwind of where the steer had been brought down. After supper, every trace of the day's camaraderie fled.

"I'm counting on the cougar returning to his kill," Matt said. "No sleep for us tonight. Good thing there will be a full moon. Check your rifles, and get in your places before it rises." He paused. "Be careful how and where you fire. We're out to get a cougar, not each other."

Josh's flesh crawled. Never in his wildest imaginings had he pictured himself lying on the ground, waiting for a mountain lion. His companions showed no signs of fear. Tracking cougars, working with ornery cattle, and hunting down rustlers were all part of their day's work. In place and invisible, they waited, with Tim motionless beside Josh. The night wore on. The moon climbed high into the sky. Josh's legs cramped from lying in one place. His nerves twanged. *Please be with us, God.* . . .

A strong hand clamped on Josh's arm and cut off the rest of the prayer. "Don't move a muscle," Tim ordered, so low Josh had to lean close to hear. "He's coming."

Josh marveled at the young man's eyesight and hearing. He strained to see and hear. A rustle in the grass and the soft *pad-pad* of footsteps rewarded his diligence. A cougar, fully five feet long and gray in the moonlight, crept toward the kill.

A shot rang out from Josh's left. *Spang!* A horrid snarl followed. The cat exploded into the air and hit the ground running.

Tim leaped to his feet and raised his rifle. "Look out, Josh. He's winged and heading our way!" With no time to take aim, he pulled the trigger. The rifle misfired. It knocked Tim to the ground, flew through the air, and landed at Josh's feet.

The enraged cougar hurled toward them — snarling, spitting, and trapping them in a nightmare from which they might never awaken.

God, help me.

Josh grabbed the rifle by the barrel and bounded to his feet, vaguely aware of shouting and the sound of men running. The cougar sprang. Josh swung the rifle with strength multiplied by fear. *Crack!* The sturdy stock smashed against the animal's head. It split in two, but it had done its work well. The mountain lion fell to the ground with one claw scraping Tim's leg. The next moment, a hail of bullets ended the predator's life.

Josh shook like an aspen leaf in a high wind. "Are you all right?" he choked out.

"I reckon." Tim struggled to his feet. "Kinda dizzy, though."

Josh looked down and gasped. Blood seeped through Tim's torn jeans. "You're hurt."

Tim's grin looked sickly in the moonlight, but he said, "Aw, it's just a scratch. Thanks to you."

"And to God." Matt forced Tim back to the ground, tore open his jeans and examined the wound. "You'll have a scar, but it looks worse than it really is." He snatched his bandana from his neck and bound Tim's leg before turning to Josh and gripping his hand until Josh winced. "It's a good thing you were here. None of us dared fire after the first shot, for fear of hitting one of you."

"Don't give me the credit," Josh protested. "I've never been so scared in my life! If God hadn't been with us . . ." The sentence died in his throat.

Matt's painful grip tightened. "Son, the

real test of a man is in taking action when he's scared to death."

The words sank into Josh's heart to be mulled over at a later time. Right now, he was too close to the near-tragedy to concentrate on anything except thanking God for sparing his and Tim's lives.

TWELVE

The staccato beat of horses' hooves the following day and Sarah's shout, "The men are home," sent Ellie flying through the ranch house doorway and toward the corral. Tim swayed in Blue's saddle, obviously in pain. Ellie saw her brother's torn, bloodstained jeans. Heart pounding, she rushed to him as Seth helped him down from the saddle.

Tim gave her a crooked smile and limped toward her. "Don't worry, Ellie. I'm fine 'cept for a love pat from a cougar who won't be killing any more stock."

"Thank God!" she burst out, throwing her arms around him.

"Yeah." Tim's smile faded, and he dropped one arm over her shoulders. "And Josh."

"Josh?" Ellie looked past Tim and met the steady gaze fixed on her.

"He saved my life."

Ellie sagged. "Saved your life!"

"Is there an echo around here?" Tim demanded. "If it hadn't been for Josh —"

"Time enough for that later," Matt snapped. "Seth, go to Madera and fetch Doc Brown."

"Not on your life!" Tim yanked free from Ellie, stumbled up the stairs onto the veranda, and dropped into a chair. "I don't need a sawbones for this little scratch. Matt already half killed me by drowning my leg with whiskey. Made me smell like a saloon." He beamed at Solita, who had stepped onto the veranda. "Solita's a good enough nurse for me. She'll fix me up."

"Si, Senor. I will bring bandages and salve." The diminutive housekeeper's eyes twinkled. "But no more whiskey."

Tim grunted. "Good. If I hadn't had witnesses, you'da thought I'd been on a spree."

Ellie's eyes filled. How typical of her brother to make light of being hurt! She clamped her lips and held back a cry of dismay when the bandage came off and exposed the wound. There was no sign of infection, but the jagged gash ran from thigh to knee: far more than a scratch.

Solita carefully examined Tim's injury. "There is no need for stitches." She cleansed the wound, plastered salve on its length, and wound it with soft linen cloths. She also ordered Tim to bed for the rest of the day.

To Ellie's surprise, her brother yawned and mumbled, "Don't mind if I do. But first, I gotta tell Ellie what Josh did." He related the moonlight incident in a few short sentences that lost none of the drama, then yawned again and allowed Matt to carry him to bed.

Ellie slipped away. She must find Josh before he left the ranch and headed back to town. She couldn't let him get away without thanking him for saving Tim. Her heartbeat tripled. The music that had begun in her soul the day of the fiesta swelled into a song of praise. She loved Joshua Stanhope. Could she face him without betraying her feelings? She knew he admired her, but was her love returned? At times, she thought so. So often when they were together, Josh's steady gaze wrapped around her like a fleecy quilt. His smile settled over her like a rainbow after a storm.

Ellie raised her chin and told her traitorous heart to be still. She hurried outside. Josh stood beside Sultan, ready to mount. Thankful that everyone else had vanished, she ran toward him. "Please wait."

Josh turned.

Ellie reached him. She clasped her hands together and willed them not to tremble.

"Josh, if it hadn't been for you, I might have lost Tim." A lump came to her throat. "How can I ever thank you?"

A beautiful light came into Josh's eyes. It softened the gray to the color of a misty dawn. He took Ellie's hands in his. "By marrying me."

Her mouth dropped. Surely she hadn't heard him right. "By . . . by . . . ," she stammered.

"Is there an echo around here?" Josh's teasing departed. "I know it's too soon. This is also not the time or place." He took in a deep breath and slowly released it. "I want you to know I've fallen in love with you, Ellie Sterling. You don't need to say anything now. Just keep this in mind: God willing, someday you'll be my beloved wife."

Josh released Ellie's hands, leaped into the saddle, and sent Sultan into a dead run. When they reached the bend in the road to Madera, he reined in, turned, and waved his sombrero. Then with a *yippee-ki-ay* worthy of Tim's best, he rode out of sight.

Ellie fled. Not to her room, where someone might discover her and want to know why she was so distraught, but to her promontory refuge. Her tumultuous heart kept time with the cadence of Calico's hooves. Josh loved her. He wanted her for his wife!

The words continued to beat in her brain as she reached the boulder on top of the promontory. Unable to contain her joy one moment longer, Ellie sat down, cupped her hands, and shouted into the valley, "Josh loves me!"

Loves me . . . loves me echoed back to her.

Ellie pressed her hands over her hot cheeks, still unable to believe it. How could a man as important as Joshua Stanhope love her? Yet he'd said, "I've fallen in love with you, Ellie Sterling."

Ellie's joy evaporated. "How will he feel when I tell him I was Ellie Stoddard for eleven years?" she asked Calico. "It looks like Gus is out of our lives, but Josh needs to know our background. Even if it doesn't make a difference to him, what about his family? What if the Lord calls Josh back to San Francisco? Would I ever fit in?"

Calico nosed her and stamped a foot as if in sympathy.

Ellie went on. "No one knows how I long to be someone, especially now. I need to be worthy of Josh's love. I'm past eighteen but all I've ever done is help around the ranch and sing in church. Tim and I have been dependent ever since we came here. It's time for me to do more." She stared down at the peaceful valley. "All Tim wants now is to ride and rope, but he may change his mind. Matt and Seth will pay for college if that's what Tim wants, but I wish I could earn money to help. I just don't know how."

The mare tossed her head and whinnied.

"I know, girl. It's time to go." Ellie mounted. "God, I'd really appreciate it if You'd . . ." her voice trailed off. She couldn't express what she wanted God to do, only that she needed Him to do something — anything — to satisfy her yearnings.

When Ellie left the promontory, she had no solution to her knotty problems. A conversation with Tim later that evening, however, brought comfort. Tim had slept most of the day and was as observant as usual. At Solita's decree, Ellie brought a supper tray to his room.

Tim wolfed down every morsel, then fixed a stern gaze on her. "You may as well spill whatever's bothering you."

"Josh asked me to marry him." Appalled at blurting out what she'd vowed to keep secret, Ellie covered her face with her hands.

Tim's fork crashed to his plate. "Great!" He frowned. "So, what's your problem? I told you Josh was a goner."

"He's in love with Ellie *Sterling,*" she

choked out.

Tim groaned. "Don't tell me you're still letting Gus spoil your life." He fell silent for a time, then added with obvious reluctance, "Besides, Josh knows Gus was our pa."

Ellie stiffened. "I suppose Luther or Amy told him."

"Naw. I did." Tim squirmed. "Don't look like that. It just came out. We were talking about cougars. I said Gus used to tell us the mountain lions would eat us if we weren't good. Josh looked disgusted and asked who Gus was. I told him, and we started talking about cougars again. Uh" — he squirmed again — "I said for him not to let on he knew 'cause you don't like being reminded about Gus."

Ellie realized her happiness depended on Tim's answer to a single question. "How did Josh take hearing we were adopted?"

Tim guffawed. "He musta taken it all right or he wouldn't have asked you to marry him." He sobered. "Josh is the best thing that ever happened to you besides our coming out here. Get it through your head that you're good enough for him or anyone."

For the second time that day, Ellie fled, hugging her brother's revelation to her heart alongside Josh's proposal. Yet the thought of not "being someone" remained.

130

Josh rode away from the Diamond S filled with disgust — not for telling Ellie he loved her, but for stupidly blurting it out next to a horse corral! No woman wanted to receive a proposal under such circumstances.

"It wasn't all my fault," Josh confided to Sultan after they rounded the bend in the road and slowed to a comfortable pace. "When Ellie looked up with those crystal blue eyes and asked how she could ever thank me, it just popped out. Know what, old boy? I'm glad she knows, even if I picked a bad time and place. Wonder how long I should wait before asking her to answer?"

The question brought him out of the clouds and back to earth. "I can't even consider it until after my six months here are up and I know where I'll be." Josh shook his head. "Luther and his hangers-on are against me because I won't confine my ministry to the members. According to Tim, Amy is all that's standing in the way of my being fired. What will she think when she finds out I'm in love with Ellie?"

Sultan snorted.

Josh's spirits rose. "My sentiments exactly!" He began to whistle and rode the rest of the way to the parsonage, watching rose-tinted clouds in the west, his mind filled with rosy dreams of a future with Ellianna Sterling.

THIRTEEN

The early September storm that slam-banged in from the Pacific Ocean paled in comparison with the fury in Charles Stanhope's face. He waved the special delivery letter that had just been delivered to him in the library. Edward had never seen his father so angry. Or heard him roar like the flames up the fireplace chimney.

"Letitia Stanhope, how dare you hire a private investigator to spy on our son?"

A wave of red mounted to her carefully styled blond hair. "You needn't shout. I did it for Joshua's sake."

Josh? Edward sagged with relief.

His mother held out her hand. "The letter's for me, is it not? Why did you open it?"

"I've been expecting to hear from our shipping office in San Diego. Thank God I opened the letter and found out what you are up to."

Curiosity overcame caution. "What does the letter say?" Edward asked.

His father cast him a quelling look but began reading:

"Except for a few malcontents at Christ the Way, Joshua has been well received. He's called 'Preacher Josh,' and people of all ages sing his praises, notably the young women who flock around him. Even in the short time he's been here, church attendance has grown substantially — especially among the ranch hands. It doesn't set well with the church chairman, but Joshua insists he must seek out those who are lost."

Edward wanted to applaud. So, good old Josh was carrying out his mission. Yet a pang went through him. He missed his twin.

His mother obviously cared little for the lost. "Just what I thought," she snapped. "A bunch of designing females making fools of themselves chasing Joshua. As if he'd ever look at anyone in that cow town."

"Don't gloat too soon." Charles gave her a stern look and resumed reading:

"According to gossip, those who plot to become Mrs. Joshua Stanhope may as well give up. The only girl your son has paid any attention to is a rancher's daughter. She sings in church and is called the Sierra Songbird. I have to admit, she has a nice voice."

Mother gave an inelegant snort. "What does an investigator know? She probably sings like a crow. Is that all?"

"Yes. Pay the investigator and dismiss him. I will have no more spying on my son. I trust him, even if you don't." He threw the letter into the fire and stalked out.

"He's my son, too," Mother flung after him. "Edward, what are we going to do?"

"Go to Madera."

A look of horror crossed her face. "You must be mad!"

Edward sat bolt upright. The idea grew like dandelions in spring. "Why not? We can find out for ourselves what's going on, meet this Sierra Songbird and" — his imagination took flight — "if she has any kind of voice, we'll bring her back with us, give her the finest training possible, and make her the rage of San Francisco. It will get her away from Josh."

Letitia wrung her hands. "You *are* mad. As mad as your brother."

"Not at all." Edward fitted his fingers

135

together and played his trump card. "When Josh left Bayview Christian, you lost the prestige of being the mother of 'our fair city's most up-and-coming minister,' as the *San Francisco Chronicle* called Josh." A gleam in his mother's eyes showed he'd reached her. She dearly loved the limelight. "There's one chance in a million that the ugly Madera duckling could turn out to be a swan. As her patron and discoverer, your social status would skyrocket."

The opposition in Mother's face gave way to consideration. "Your father won't hear of it." Her regretful voice told Edward he'd won.

He stood and stretched. "He'd do anything to help make peace between you and Josh. What's more effective than our visiting Madera and offering the local songbird a chance to soar?" Edward shrugged. "Who knows? It might even cause Josh to reconsider where he's supposed to be. Bayview Christian's still holding his place open, aren't they?"

"Yes." A conspiratorial look passed between mother and son.

Three days later Letitia and Edward ferried to Oakland and boarded the eastbound train.

Josh thrust aside the sermon he'd been working on and headed for the Diamond S. "The only honorable thing to do is confess to Matt," he told Sultan. The black gelding pricked his ears into the listening attitude Josh knew so well. "How could I take advantage of Ellie when she was distraught over Tim?"

He repeated the question in Matt's office a short time later. Matt sat behind his desk with Josh standing across from him, feeling like a prisoner before a judge. "Ellie asked me what she could do to thank me for saving Tim." Sweat crawled up Josh's back. "I blurted out 'by marrying me.'"

Matt's voice cut like a skinning knife. "Did you mean it?"

Josh clenched his fists. "I never meant anything more."

Matt crossed his arms and tilted his desk chair back until it groaned. "So what's the problem?"

Josh swallowed, wishing he was anywhere else. "I should have told you how I felt and asked permission to keep company with Ellie before speaking out like that."

"Did you tell Ellie you love her and ask

her how she feels?"

Josh felt himself turn pale. "You sure aren't making this easy. Not that I deserve anything else."

"What do you expect?" The chair crashed down on all fours. "A man comes to me, says he told my only daughter she could marry him because he happened to be in the right place at the right time, and —"

The words stung. Josh stepped forward and glared down at Matt. "It's not like that, Matt. I didn't ask anything from Ellie except for her to keep in mind that someday, God willing, she'll be my beloved wife." He met his friend's stern blue gaze squarely. "We've known each other a little less than three months. I'm twenty-seven. She's eighteen. I wouldn't expect her to love me now, although sometimes . . ." His voice lay down and died.

Mischief replaced the sternness in Matt's eyes. He got up from behind the desk, wearing a Cheshire-cat grin. One strong hand shot out and gripped Josh's. "Put her there, Preacher Josh. You may have my daughter's hand in marriage if you can win her. In the meantime, see that Tim 'keeps company' with you two unless you're in a crowd." His mirth changed to sadness. "Ellie was the target of vicious gossip as a child. It left scars. There's at least one two-legged cat in the vicinity who will scratch and squall if she thinks you're serious about Ellie."

"I know." Josh heaved a great sigh. "Tim already warned me that Amy Talbot has been making her intentions known all over town."

"It figures." Matt gave Josh a lopsided grin. "One thing. How will that San Francisco family of yours feel about Ellie?"

Josh's joy evaporated, but he wouldn't duck Matt's question. "My father will have reservations only until he meets her, Mother will huff and puff and try to blow my house down but will have to give in. My twin brother, Edward, will —"

"Twin brother! There are two of you?"

The look on Matt's face proved too much for Josh. He bent double laughing. "That bad, huh?"

Matt dropped back into his chair and stared until Josh felt impaled by his keen gaze. "No. It's just that I've heard twins sometimes share the same feelings." Matt cleared his throat and looked uncomfortable. "If your brother is like you, what's to keep him from falling in love with Ellie when he meets her? I'd hate to see her in a tug-of-war between brothers. Bad business. All three of you would lose."

Matt's insight sent a chill through Josh. "We look alike, but it ends there. Edward and I chose different paths in life a long time ago. Besides, he's already engaged." *Right,* a little voice taunted. *Beryl Westfield is like a burned-out comet compared with Ellie, who brings the sunlight. How can Edward or any man help falling in love with her? You were down for the count the first time you met her.*

"Well?"

Josh gathered his wits and replied, "Edward may have his faults, but I'm sure he has enough honor to never come between me and the woman I love."

Are you sure? the little voice persisted. *Absolutely sure?* Josh wanted to drown out the voice with a resounding yes, but doubts born of past experience rose. If push came to shove, would Edward let anything stand between him and something he'd set his mind on possessing? Time after time, the role of brother's keeper had lain heavy on Josh's shoulders. He'd given up much for Edward. If he fell in love with Ellie, as Josh knew could happen, must the older brother stand aside in order to keep Ellie from becoming a wishbone?

Matt leaned forward. "You can take my advice or not, Josh. But if I were you, I'd

140

get a ring on Ellie's finger before that brother of yours ever meets her."

Josh's mouth dried. "A wedding ring?" His heart leaped at the thought.

Matt rolled his eyes. "No, you dolt. A brand. A sparkler. An engagement ring. Something to tell the world she belongs to you."

"You're all right with that?" Josh marveled.

Matt cocked one eyebrow and drawled, "Well now, Preacher, it really isn't up to me. One thing more. How are you going to support my daughter if Luther Talbot convinces folks you need to mosey on three months from now? I doubt you've saved much on the salary you get here."

Josh wanted to laugh. "I have income from a trust fund my grandfather left and saved quite a bit from Bayview Christian. The trust fund principal comes to me when I'm thirty, unless Mother finds a way to stop it. She didn't want me to leave San Francisco. By the way, this is privileged information."

"Of course." Matt's eyes twinkled. He stood, signaling the interview had ended. "You're a good rider. If Talbot succeeds in getting you kicked out, which I'm pretty sure he won't, I can always use another good hand."

"Thanks. I'll keep it in mind. Now I'd best

be getting back to town before Luther sends a pack of hounds after me."

"He's about ready to," Matt warned. "His big gripe continues to be that you spend way too much time outside the church and parsonage."

"How do you feel about it?" Josh asked.

"You have to do both. Tend the flock and go after the strays."

Josh told Matt good-bye and headed back to Madera, pondering over the remarkable session and thinking of the rancher's final words. So much to do. If only there were more hours in a day! "There aren't," Josh told Sultan. "Hmmm. Wonder what's next?"

He didn't have long to wait. The eastbound train was grinding to a stop when Josh reached Madera. He tethered Sultan to the hitching rail in front of Moore's General Store and idly watched passengers descend to the dusty street. A heavily veiled woman paused on the platform at the top of the steps, with the porter attempting to assist her. A haughty voice commanded, "My good man, I can walk. Will you please let go of my elbow?"

Blood rushed to Josh's head and roared in his ears. The voice could only belong to one person. "Mother?" he croaked.

Letitia stepped down, followed by her

grinning younger son. "Really Joshua, must you gape?" She cast a disparaging glance up and down Main Street. "That's what comes of living in a place like this. Now, will you kindly take me somewhere so I can recover from our dreadful journey?"

She looked at the well-filled horse trough nearby and sniffed. "I presume there are accommodations with modern conveniences. Or is this where people here bathe?"

FOURTEEN

"Mother!" Josh grabbed the woman's arm. He helped her from the street to the sidewalk that ran in front of the store, wishing the wooden planks beneath his feet would open and swallow him. He sent Edward a silent cry for help, but his twin had obviously been rendered speechless by their mother's rude remark. *Why are they here?* Josh wondered. *How can Mother, with all her social graces, be so insufferable? What is she trying to do, make me a laughingstock and undermine my work in Madera so I'll have to go home? The sooner I can get her out of here, the better.*

Before Josh could steer Letitia away, an elderly man hobbled his way through the crowd that always gathered to meet the trains. His cracked voice grated on Josh's ears. "Jumpin' jackrabbits, are there two preachers here or am I seein' double?" He shook his head as if to clear it. "Can't be. I ain't had a drink for nigh onto ten years."

This cannot be happening, Josh thought in despair. *It's like something out of a bad dream.* "You're all right," Josh said aloud. "Mother, Edward, this is my friend Dan Doyle."

Dan dipped his head to Josh's mother. "Pleased to meetcha, ma'am. You got a mighty fine son here. T'other one looks toler'ble, too." He cackled and held out a gnarled hand.

Mother ignored it, but Edward quickly reached out. "Thank you, Mr. Doyle."

Dan swelled with pride. Josh bit back a guffaw. *Bless Edward.* The old man probably hadn't been called *Mister* for years, if ever.

Edward turned to his brother. "About accommodations . . ."

Josh led his mother away before she could blurt out another derogatory remark. "It's just a short way to the Yosemite Hotel. You'll be comfortable there. By the way, where's Father?"

Mother made a sour face. "Traveling to San Diego on business." She fell mercifully silent, but Josh inwardly cringed. Her expression showed total contempt for Madera. On the other hand, Edward looked amused, even interested.

"It's rather picturesque, isn't it?" he exclaimed while they walked down Main Street. When they reached the Yosemite Hotel he stopped short and gazed at the imposing brick building. "Nothing wrong with that, Mother."

"It isn't too bad," she conceded.

Josh squelched the desire to tell her that years earlier before the original structure burned, Mace's Hotel had been a tiny wooden shanty that served as a saloon as well as a lodging place.

She stopped short and stared up the street. "Who is *that*?" She pointed to a bearded man leading a spirited horse. Dressed in a fine suit and tie, the man carried a gold-handled cane. A top hat completed the picture of elegance.

Josh battled the desire to repay his mother for humiliating him — and lost. "The captain."

She looked blank.

"Captain Russell Perry Mace. He's a hero. He hunted buffalo with Kit Carson, was wounded in the Mexican-American War, and spent years searching for gold before helping to establish Madera. He also served in the California State Legislature."

"Dear me, why would such a fine gentleman live in this godforsaken place?"

"The captain owns the Yosemite Hotel," Josh quietly said. "And God hasn't forsaken Madera, Mother. He sent me here." The instant the words left his mouth, he regretted them. Who was he to contradict his mother? Fortunately, her attention was so fixed on the captain that she either didn't hear or chose to ignore her son.

Edward snickered. "You'll have something to boast about to your friends, Mother. Meeting a hero and all that."

The captain reached them before she could reply. "Well, well, who do we have here?" He looked from Josh to Edward. "Twins, is it?" He didn't wait for a reply but turned to Letitia. "You, madam, must be their proud mother." He beamed at Letitia, who looked completely bowled over.

"Yes. I'm Mrs. Stanhope and this is Edward."

"Good. Good." The captain rubbed his hands. "Preacher Josh's coming to Madera is the best thing that's happened around here for a long time. I take it you and Edward will be staying at my hotel, Mrs. Stanhope? I'll be honored if you'll join me for supper. You, too, Preacher. Six thirty?"

Josh hoped his mother wouldn't blurt out that they usually dined much later. He sighed with relief when she merely said,

147

"We'll be happy to join you, Captain Mace. Six thirty is fine."

"Good," he trumpeted. "Come in, and make yourselves at home." He led the way into the richly furnished foyer with its impressive staircase leading to the upstairs sleeping chambers. Mother's eyes widened, and her mouth fell open. Clearly, she hadn't expected this.

"Joshua, do you have rooms here?"

"No. I live in the parsonage next to the church." He glanced down at his dusty clothes. "I'll stable Sultan, get cleaned up, and meet you here." He beat a hasty retreat, his heart lighter than it had been since his family arrived. Thanks to the opportune appearance of the colorful Captain Mace, maybe things would be all right.

Just before the outer door of the hotel swung shut, he heard his mother ask, "Do we dress for din— supper?"

"Some do. Some don't," the captain replied. "Wear what you like."

Josh chuckled to himself and hurried back to care for Sultan. How would Mother react to eating in the same room with sheepmen and cowboys, travelers, shopkeepers, and their wives? He shrugged. He could do nothing about it, except leave it to the Lord. But again Josh wondered, *Why are Mother and Edward here?*

He continued to wonder during the superlative dinner in the well-appointed dining room. Gaslight flickered on crystal and china. It gleamed on silver cutlery and tablecloths as starched and spotless as the pinafore-style aprons the waitresses wore. Josh rejoiced in the young women's usual efficient service. His mother could have no complaint about it, even though she looked askance at their fellow diners.

The captain took center stage. Josh had heard some of his stories before but enjoyed the talkative hotel proprietor's confession that gold mining wasn't all it was cracked up to be. "One day, I washed thirty-four buckets of dirt in the forenoon and made sixty-two and one-half cents. In the afternoon, I bought a sack of flour, a half pound of pork, and a dollar's worth of soap. It cost eight dollars."

Mother eyed him suspiciously, but Edward's eyes sparkled. Unless Josh was badly mistaken, his brother was having the time of his life.

When the last bite of the Lady Baltimore cake had vanished, the captain shoved his chair back from the table. "I imagine I'll see you in church tomorrow, especially Pastor Josh." He laughed heartily.

Josh held his breath, but Edward nodded. So did Mother.

"Good. Thank you for having supper with me." The captain pulled out Mother's chair. When she rose, he nodded and strolled out of the dining room.

Josh felt at a loss as to what to do next. "Would you like to see my parsonage?" he finally asked.

"Not tonight. I'm going to my room." His mother swept out, long skirts trailing behind her.

Thud. Josh's hopes fell to his toes. He turned to face Edward. "Is she ever going to forgive me?"

An unreadable expression came into his twin's eyes, an expression that left Josh uneasy without knowing why. "She's here, isn't she?"

Yet a question hammered in Josh's brain: *True — but what does it mean?*

After a sleepless night spent reviewing the sermon he'd planned, Josh gave it up at dawn. "Sorry, Lord. With Mother and Edward in the congregation, I simply can't preach about the Lost Son." He buried his head in his hands. "What shall I do?"

Silence followed. Peace came, first as a trickle, then like a river. It brought the feeling all would be well. Josh grabbed writing tools and began making notes.

A few hours later, he stepped behind the pulpit of Christ the Way, opened his Bible, and announced, "Our text today is from John 14." Pages rustled as the congregation found the place. Josh's heart thundered when he said, "Jesus told His disciples in verse 1, *'Let not your heart be troubled: ye believe in God, believe also in me.'* In verse 27, He said, *'Peace I leave with you, my peace I give unto you: not as the world giveth, give I unto you. Let not your heart be troubled, neither let it be afraid.'* "

He paused and closed the Bible. "Instead of preaching a regular sermon this morning, I'm going to tell you the story of a remarkable man." He heard a snort from behind him. *Please, God, don't let Luther Talbot make a scene.* Josh straightened. He wouldn't give the chairman a chance.

"Horatio Spafford and his wife lived in Chicago. They had four daughters, who ranged from eighteen months in age to twelve years. In the winter of 1873, the family joyously looked forward to a trip to Europe. The time for the trip grew close, but business difficulties forced Spafford to remain at home. Unwilling to deprive his family of the trip, he kissed them good-bye,

151

bade them Godspeed, and promised to join them as soon as possible.

"Anna Spafford and the girls boarded a French steamer and began their journey. Tragedy struck off the coast of Newfoundland. The ship collided with an English sailing vessel, which ripped a huge hole in the *Ville de Havre*'s hull. It plunged to the bottom of the ocean within twenty minutes.

"Just before the ship sank, Anna gathered her girls and prayed. The icy North Atlantic swept over them. It took the three oldest girls, then snatched the baby from her mother's arms. Alone and near death, Anna was rescued by those in a lifeboat. Ten anxious days passed before the survivors landed in Wales. Anna wired her husband:

SAVED ALONE.

Heartbroken, Horatio boarded the next available ship to England and was reunited with Anna. They returned to Chicago."

Josh paused and looked from face to face. "How many times does our faith weaken when we face adversity? Who among us could face such a loss and remain steadfast? My mother and brother are here today. I don't know what I'd do if I ever lost either of them or my father. Yet the Spaffords trusted God and kept the faith. Horatio later returned to where the *Ville de Havre* went down. A hymn came out of his pain."

Not a sound could be heard in the entire church. Josh saw tears trembling on his mother's eyelashes. Edward sat as if turned to stone. *Thank You, Lord.*

Josh looked at Ellie. Her glowing eyes reflected her love for the God who had delivered her and Tim from a life of sadness. "I've asked Miss Sterling to sing 'It Is Well with My Soul,' the song wrenched from Horatio Spafford's heart by tragedy."

Ellie slowly stepped forward. Abby struck a single note on the organ and stopped playing. Ellie clasped her hands against her pale yellow gown and began to sing:

"When peace, like a river, attendeth my
   way,
When sorrows like sea billows roll;
Whatever my lot, Thou has taught me to
   say,
It is well, it is well with my soul."

The glorious voice soared with triumph, needing no accompaniment:

"It is well . . . with my soul . . .
It is well, it is well with my soul."

Josh looked at Edward. Clearly astonished, his brother straightened in his seat and fixed his gaze on Ellie. So did Mother. The song continued. Josh saw his brother whisper to their mother. A satisfied smile appeared, but she never took her attention from Ellie.

"It is well . . . with my soul . . .
It is well, it is well with my soul."

Ellie had never sung so magnificently. Josh had never loved her more. Why then, did foreboding fill him? Another quick glance at his mother increased his apprehension. Whenever she looked like a pussycat who'd plundered the cream pitcher, it meant trouble. The unpleasant suspicion that his mother and Edward were neck-deep in some nefarious scheme perched on Josh's shoulder and clawed into him.

If not, why were they here?

FIFTEEN

Josh barely got the final *amen* out before his mother and Edward left their seats and rushed up the aisle to Ellie. Letitia laid her gloved hand on the girl's arm and beamed. Josh hadn't seen her so fluttery since the mayor of San Francisco presented her with what Edward called a "do-gooder" award for work with various city charities.

"My *dear,*" she gushed, "what a *marvel*-ous voice! And that song . . ." She dabbed at her eyes with her handkerchief and turned to Matt and his family. "You must be the Sterlings. Surely you are proud of this young lady." Her treble voice rang through the church.

Tim gawked. Ellie blinked. Sarah's eyes twinkled. The corners of Matt's mouth twitched as he said, "And you must be Mrs. Stanhope and Edward." He held out his hand. "I'm glad you came."

Josh wished he could say the same. It

might be unjust, but he couldn't rid himself of the feeling mischief was brewing.

"Mr. and Mrs. Sterling, will you and your family be our guests for lunch at the Yosemite Hotel?" Edward laughed and corrected himself. "Dinner, that is."

"Thank you," Matthew said. "Sarah, Tim, Ellie, and I will be happy to accept. Our younger children can go home with my sister and her husband."

Edward gave them his most charming smile. "I'm sure Josh will be joining us."

You can bet on it, Brother. I'm not letting you and Mother out of my sight until you're back on the train to San Francisco. Josh left the platform and came to the group. "Of course. Let's step outside. Folks will want to meet you." He maneuvered them down the aisle and into the yard. His heart warmed to the way the congregation flocked around his family. But when Amy Talbot, wearing a fluffy lilac gown and a here-I-go-a-hunting look approached Edward, Josh wanted to howl with mirth.

Wide-eyed and innocent, she peered up into Edward's face, then clapped her small hands. "I declare, you really are alike as two peas in a pod." Amy giggled. "What a blessing to have two such handsome men in church today!" She batted her eyelashes.

"You know, Mr. Stanhope, we're all simply crazy about your brother. If you plan to stay for a few days, Father and I would love to entertain you. I'm Amy Talbot, and my father is chairman of the church board."

If looks could kill, Josh judged, *Amy would be dead at Mother's small feet.* She started to reply, but was drowned out by Tim's hoarse laugh. Josh saw Ellie elbow him, and Tim changed it to a fit of coughing; Josh's sentiments exactly.

Edward, suave as usual, shook his head. "I'm afraid we'll have to turn down your invitation, Miss Talbot. We'll be returning to San Francisco as soon as we finish our business here."

Business? What business? Josh's premonition of storm clouds lurking just beyond the closest hill increased with Edward's almost imperceptible nod to his mother.

The crowd began to disperse. Amy and her father, who had unbent long enough to be introduced to the Stanhopes, lingered, obviously in hopes of being included in the dinner invitation. They didn't leave until Tim broadly hinted, "If we don't mosey along to the hotel, we may not be able to all sit together."

Luther cast him a withering look. "Come, Amy." He started off. Amy flounced after him, but turned and called back, "Don't forget! If you decide to stay longer, my invitation still holds," then tripped after her rigid father.

"Whew! Is this what preachers have to put up with?" Edward asked. "Glad I didn't become one. What do you think, Miss Sterling? Is everyone here really crazy about my brother?" He offered his arm.

Ellie sent Josh a pleading glance before placing her fingertips on Edward's arm. "Not everyone. But Tim is right. We'd best be on our way."

"Mother?" Josh held out his arm, seething inside. What audacity! He lowered his voice. "Why are you and Edward here?"

Her cat-in-the-cream expression returned. "For your own good, Joshua." She refused to elaborate on the walk to the hotel.

Dinner seemed endless in spite of the banter that flowed around Josh. Ellie and Sarah said little; Tim, nothing at all. Edward and Mother dominated the conversation, extolling the wonders of San Francisco but always coming back to Ellie's singing. One by one, the other diners left. When only the Sterlings and Stanhopes remained, Mother turned to Matt and delivered a verbal blow. "Edward and I had a reason for coming to Madera other than seeing Joshua." She tapped her fingers on the table. "We want permission to kidnap your daughter."

Josh's first thought left him shaking. *Matt was right. I should have gotten a ring on Ellie's finger before she met Edward.* The next moment, the full impact of the plot struck him. It took all of Josh's control to keep from raging at his mother. He set his teeth in his lower lip and tasted blood, the only way to hold back words that once spoken, would haunt him forever.

Sarah gasped. Ellie sat as if frozen. Tim uttered a smothered protest, flung his napkin to the table, and leaped to his feet.

Matt straightened in his chair. His eyes turned midnight blue. "I beg your pardon?" Icicles dripped from his voice.

Edward stepped into the breach. "I'm sorry Mother was so blunt." He sounded sincere, but from long experience, Josh knew better.

"We don't really want to kidnap her." Edward leaned forward, and his eyes gleamed. "We want to take Miss Sterling to San Francisco and give her the finest musical training available. Josh told us how well the Sierra Songbird sings. Hearing her this morning in church confirms his opinion. Think of the good your daughter can do. We have the ability to help her become the toast of San Francisco and make a fortune. This is also a once-in-a-lifetime opportunity to touch lives with her God-given talent —"

"She's already doing that!" Tim interrupted, hands clenched in a fighting stance. "You think folks here come to church just to hear Preacher Josh?" His voice rose. "They don't. They also come to hear Ellie sing. You may be our preacher's mother and brother, but you've got some nerve showing up and trying to take Ellie away from us!"

"Sit down, Tim," Matt ordered. His eyes flashed fire. "I should apologize for my son, but I won't. He said exactly what I'm thinking. Unless I'm sadly mistaken, Josh feels the same way."

All eyes turned toward Josh. He started to speak, then caught sight of Ellie's face. She hadn't moved since Mother had fired the opening salvo in what surely would be a relentless war to get her own way . . . and the Sierra Songbird. A quick look at Mother's tightly buttoned mouth showed how long and hard that battle would be.

Josh jerked his attention back to Ellie. Every trace of color had left her cheeks. Her lips trembled. Her eyes looked enormous. He started to agree with Tim and Matt, but something in Ellie's face stopped him: a wistful expression that showed Edward's plea had kindled a spark. *Tread lightly.*

The unspoken admonition curbed Josh's tongue. "Ellie?"

Obviously distraught, she stood so abruptly that her chair crashed to the floor, then ran out of the dining room.

Josh rounded on Edward. "How could you?"

He raised one eyebrow. "This doesn't concern you, Josh. It's between Miss Sterling and her parents."

"And her brother," Tim reminded.

"Of course." Edward rose and helped their mother to her feet. "Why don't we go to our rooms and give you a chance to find the lady involved and think it over?"

"If we think it over until Judgment Day, you still can't have Ellie," Tim growled. "I gotta go find her." He raced out.

Mother, who had remained silent during the encounter, smiled and patted Sarah's hand. "I'm sorry, dear, it's just that we have your daughter's welfare at heart. Her chances here are quite limited. You mustn't be selfish and hold her back."

Josh had never in his life come so close to disliking his mother. Couldn't she see what she'd done? She and Edward had shot the day to smithereens. Not trusting himself to speak, he went to find the girl he loved.

■ ■ ■ ■

When Ellie left the dining room, she fled to the place in Madera that offered refuge: Christ the Way Church. Knowing she'd be pursued, she ducked behind buildings and through the alley instead of staying on Main Street, where she could be spotted. Yet once she reached the church, she reconsidered. It was the first place they'd look for her. She needed time alone to grasp everything that had happened.

A large oak tree a little distance away offered sanctuary. Ellie sped toward it and sank to the ground beneath its sheltering branches. The day's events whirled through her mind, starting when Tim had helped her down from the buggy in front of the church. . . .

"Hurry or we'll be late." Ellie's heart sang as usual, knowing she'd soon see Josh. She and Tim went inside and found their places. A slight stir at the back of the church caused heads to swivel. Ellie blinked. Why was Josh sitting down beside a middle-aged blond woman wearing the most stylish hat that had been seen in Madera in years? He should be up front sitting beside frowning Luther Talbot, who insisted on occupying a seat on the platform during each service.

Tim poked Ellie. "Who's the fancy dame? Where'd Josh get the duded-up suit?"

Ellie shook her head and turned toward the front of the church.

"It ain't Josh after all," Tim reported, head still craned toward the back row. "He's just now coming through the door. The other guy's gotta be Josh's twin. Betcha the woman's their mother."

Ellie gulped. Had Josh mentioned her to his family? Had they come to look her over? She pushed the thought aside and concentrated on the service. When Josh finished the story of Horatio Stafford and beckoned to her, she stepped forward. She forgot about Josh's family until she sang the last line of her song, "It is well, it is well with my soul." She breathed a silent prayer of thanks and discovered a pair of gray eyes identical to the young minister's steadily regarding her. No, not identical. The new-comer's gaze held impudence. Josh's did not.

Ellie returned to her seat like one in a trance. She suffered Mrs. Stanhope's and Amy's gushing, Edward's invitation, and the walk to the Yosemite Hotel with the wrong brother. Charming he might be, but he wasn't Josh. Ellie wished with all her heart that he would trade places with Edward. And when Mrs. Stanhope said, "We want permission to kidnap your daughter," Ellie wondered if the woman was quite mad.

Now she buried her face in her hands. Snatches from the glowing picture Edward had painted sank into her soul. *Finest musical training available . . . the good your daughter can do . . . the ability to help her become the toast of San Francisco . . . make a fortune . . . once-in-a-lifetime opportunity . . . touch lives with her God-given talent.*

Ellie slipped to her knees. "Please help me, God. I can't leave Josh! He loves me and wants me for his wife. That's what I want, too." Yet her traitorous heart clamored to be heard. With a cry of despair, Ellie confessed, "Lord, I've asked You for years to help me be someone. No one but You knows how much I want to be worthy of Josh. Could this be Your answer? The Diamond S has been like the end of the rainbow, but do You have greater treasure waiting for me in San Francisco?"

Her heart beat faster. "What if everything Edward describes comes true? I could serve You and save money to provide for Tim instead of being beholden to Matt and Seth. I could also become someone Josh would be proud of no matter where You lead Him.

Besides, it's not like it would be forever."

Ellie raised her head. She looked at the church. She thought of her family and life on the ranch. Sobs wracked her slender body. How could she bear to give up all she knew and loved? Yet she'd asked for an opportunity to be someone. What if God was calling her to the city the way He'd called Josh to Madera? How could she accept? How could she refuse?

SIXTEEN

Josh gritted his teeth and marched through the front door of the Yosemite Hotel. If he stayed in the dining room one minute more, he would erupt like a volcano and say words that could never be recalled. How dare Mother patronize Sarah and accuse her of selfishly holding Ellie back? Church members and nonmembers alike heaped praise on Sarah. They obviously considered her one of the finest women in the valley, and according to Red Fallon, Sarah was a true angel of forgiveness. As for Edward, Josh's anger burned hotter with every step.

He caught sight of Tim loping down Main Street ahead of him. "Wait up," Josh called. Tim glanced back, paused, and waited. A white line around the boy's tightly closed mouth and the lightning that flickered in his eyes warned of an impending storm. It broke when Josh reached him.

"Your brother's not much like you, is he?"

Tim burst out. "You'd never come up with a fool idea like taking Ellie to San Francisco."

"No." A world of regret poured into Josh's reply and a look of understanding passed between them. "Not that she isn't talented enough. She is. Edward's right about that, but high society is no place for Ellie. She's far too unsophisticated for the circles in which Mother and Edward travel."

Fear darkened Tim's eyes until they looked almost black. "Yeah, but Ellie may not think so." He kicked at the road, and swirls of yellow dust rose. "Did you see her face when your brother was spouting about this being her big opportunity? And then she ran out! I wanted to hit your brother for making her look like that."

"So did I," Josh confessed. "I wish he and Mother had never come to Madera."

"Same here. I'm afraid Ellie may fall for all that stuff. Come on. We gotta find her." Tim cocked his head to one side. "She probably went back to the church." He started on, easily keeping pace with Josh's long strides. "Hey, I guess being a preacher doesn't stop you from getting mad, does it?"

"No." Josh produced a feeble grin. "It just keeps me from hitting folks!"

Tim grunted but fell silent. Josh suspected that for once he didn't have a reply.

When they reached Christ the Way, Josh warned, "We need to go in quietly. If Ellie's praying, we don't want to bother her." He opened the door, and they stepped inside. Only silence from the empty room greeted them.

Tim looked wise. "When things bother Ellie, she likes to go off by herself. She probably figured the church is the first place we'd look for her. We'll find her outside somewhere."

It didn't take long to discover Ellie's refuge. Josh spotted her beneath the huge oak tree, a yellow-clad figure drooping in a way that tore at his heart. Unwilling to interrupt her solitude, he put his finger to his lips and motioned Tim back. They retreated to the church steps and waited without speaking. Josh could sense waves of pain and helplessness coming from the boy beside him. Tim stood on the brink of manhood, ready to leave his little-brother role and become Ellie's protector.

Josh longed to offer words of comfort, but they stuck in his throat. Edward and Mother had stirred Ellie's interest, or she wouldn't have run away to be alone. What would it mean to his future with the girl he loved?

Could she withstand the persuasiveness of Letitia and Edward Stanhope, the lure of adulation?

Josh tried to brush aside his anxiety, but it stuck to him like a hungry mosquito. So did doubts about Edward. Josh had seen the astonished delight in his brother's face when Ellie sang. Edward knew and loved good music. He could have been an accomplished pianist if he'd cared enough to practice instead of chasing after other interests. Would loyalty to his twin overcome the impact of Ellie's freshness and innocence while Edward helped her climb to the pinnacle of success? Josh closed his eyes and silently prayed, *Not my will but Thine be done.*

At last Ellie rose and came toward them. Her tear-stained face bore mute witness to her inner turmoil. Love for Josh shone clear and true in her beautiful eyes, but she had obviously been deeply affected by his family's proposition.

Letitia and Edward Stanhope extended their stay at the Yosemite Hotel. They suffered the twenty-mile round-trip to the ranch and back to plead with the Sterlings to allow Ellie to accompany them back to the city. They again pointed out the advantages Ellie would have. She felt like a wishbone, torn between clinging to the security of the life she knew and loved and the life the Stanhopes offered — most of all, the chance to be someone and make a difference in the lives of others. Prayer brought little peace. She wavered between saying no outright and agreeing to go for a short time.

The turmoil created by the Stanhopes' persistence didn't end with Ellie. Or with Tim or Josh, drawn together by common concern. It profoundly affected the Diamond S family and friends. Matt, Sarah, and Seth adamantly opposed Ellie's going to San Francisco. To Ellie's amazement, Seth's wife, Dori, firmly disagreed.

"Remember when I just had to go to school in Boston?" she asked Matt early one evening in the sitting room before the fire when the discussion raged hot and heavy. Ellie sat in a shadowy corner at one side, listening without speaking.

Her brother made a face. "Do I ever! Do you remember how you hated it?"

Dori tossed her dark curls. "Do I ever!" she mimicked, bright blue eyes shining. "Even though it became a disaster, I'm glad I went."

"Why?" Tim demanded from his spot on the floor in front of the fire.

Dori sobered. "I had to go away in order to appreciate what I have here." She smiled at Seth. "I have a feeling Ellie will do the same."

He shook his head and looked troubled. "After the freedom of living on the ranch, I'm afraid she will be like a wild bird in a cage."

It felt strange being discussed as if she were not present, yet Ellie remained silent and allowed the talk to flow around her.

Solita spoke for the first time since the conversation began. For once, her timeworn brown hands lay idle in her lap. "If our Sierra Songbird goes to the city and *Dios* does not wish her to remain, no bars will hold her." She turned to Ellie, and her black eyes softened. "Senorita, what does your heart say?"

The moment of truth Ellie had dreaded ever since the Stanhopes dangled the promise of fame and fortune before her lay heavy in the quiet room. Only the crackle of the fire and the happy laughter of children at play outside the front door broke the silence.

Ellie clenched her hands until the nails bit into her palms. Tears sneaked past her eyelids. She knew they left glistening tracks on their journey down her cheeks. Her voice came out barely above a whisper. "I've prayed and prayed about it. I don't want to leave you and the ranch, but I feel like I must go." It was out, the words she'd known must be said but that would change her life, perhaps forever.

Tim, who had been unusually quiet during the exchange, leaped to his feet and glared at her. "For crying out loud, are you crazy? What about Josh? The minute you leave, Amy will be —"

"Tim!" Matt interrupted. "That's enough. We appreciate how you feel, but this has to be Ellie's decision: no one else's."

Tim gave him a rebellious look and stalked out. Ellie put her hands over her burning face, glad for her dimly lit corner. But Tim's question refused to be ignored. What about Josh? Just this afternoon Matt had called Ellie aside and repeated the interview in which Josh confessed his feelings and received permission to keep company with her.

"He's only been here a short time, but I believe Josh loves you the way I love Sarah," Matt had said. "He's a fine man, Ellie. You'll never do better."

Now, still ecstatic over Matt's affirmation, Ellie's decision to leave Madera faltered once more. How could she go hundreds of miles away into a new and perhaps frightening world when the love she wanted more than life itself remained in Madera? The next moment she steadied her churning mind. Surely Josh's love — and hers — could endure a short separation. Besides, as Solita said, if God didn't want Ellie to stay in San Francisco she could come home as Dori had.

The thought comforted her. *I truly believe You want me to go, Lord,* she prayed that night while lying in bed and looking out the window at the winking stars. *It's my chance to become worthy of Josh. And to rid myself forever of the stigma of being Gus Stoddard's daughter.* She fell asleep, dreaming of cattle and cable cars, cowboys and creek beds, and the clang of the city the Stanhopes had described.

The dream changed to an all-too-familiar nightmare, but one Ellie hadn't had for years. The sounds of San Francisco and the San Joaquin Valley changed to childish voices, taunting and cruel: *"You ain't nothing, Ellianna Stoddard. Neither's your Pa. Trash, that's what you are — and you ain't never gonna be nothin' else."*

The cry of a coyote awakened Ellie, mocking as the voices in her dream. Instead of the sickening feeling that had always followed the dream, however, determination flooded through her. "You're wrong about me," she fiercely whispered to the haunting voices. "With God's help, I'll show you, San Francisco — and the world."

Her mind raced. Her purpose grew. "I'm going to work hard and become everything Edward and Mrs. Stanhope promised: rich, famous, and a blessing to others. I had enough trouble as a child to be called Job's granddaughter. This is my chance to have people look up to me, not down on me. I will learn to be a wife of whom Josh can be proud."

When Ellie again fell asleep, no dreams troubled her. She awoke resolved to carry out the vow she had made in the night hours — and sent word to the Stanhopes she was willing to leave Madera.

Two days later Ellie shook the dust of her past off her new, stylish boots and left for San Francisco with Mrs. Stanhope and Edward.

Ellie bade Josh a heart-wrenching goodbye. When he clasped her hands as if he'd never let her go, Ellie wanted to fling herself into his arms, regardless of the crowd at the station. Only the desire to become worthy of the unguarded love shining in Josh's eyes kept Ellie true to her course. The last thing she saw when the train wheels began their *clackety-clack* to carry her away was Josh waving from the steps of Christ the Way Church. Tim stood beside him, somber faced and with arms crossed.

Ellie's vision blurred. For one wild moment, she longed to cry out, "Stop the train!" Instead, she raised her chin, set her face toward the west, and didn't look back.

Seventeen

Ellie glanced around the passenger coach. She stifled a giggle, but her eyes stung. How different this was from the common car in which she and Tim had huddled on their trip from St. Louis to California! She closed her eyes and pictured two frightened children facing an unknown future. There had been no gingerbread trimmings, no polished brass lamps hanging from the ceiling. Certainly no stained-glass transoms to reflect rainbow colors across the rich, plush seats.

She thought of the dining car with its spotless white tablecloths and well-trained attendants. She and Tim had been too timid to even sneak a peek into the dining car when they came to Madera. Ellie forced the comparisons out of her mind. *That was then. This is now.*

"Well, we're on our way," Edward said.

His laugh and resemblance to Josh sent a

twinge through Ellie. *Oh dear! Only a few miles lie between the speeding train and home, and I'm already missing Josh. This will never do.* She dismissed the thought and put on a bright smile. "Yes."

Mrs. Stanhope settled herself more firmly in her seat. "We need to talk about you, Ellie." She raised one eyebrow. "The first thing we'll do when we get home is take you to a good hairdresser and *modiste.*" She gave Ellie's well-cut traveling gown a nod of approval. "Your clothing is fine for Madera, but San Francisco fashion demands —"

"Hang San Francisco fashion!" Edward cut in. "You're not going to turn the Sierra Songbird into a bird of paradise."

Ellie gaped, unable to believe her own ears, but Edward wasn't through.

"Look at Ellie, Mother. See how her hair curls under at the nape of her neck? And the way her soft bangs curve across her forehead? It makes her look like a page from the days of knights and ladies." His eyes sparkled. "When she sings, she must wear simple, tunic-style dresses that highlight her uniqueness."

Mrs. Stanhope bridled, and her mouth set in a stubborn line. "As if you know about fashion and the proper dress for ladies!"

"I know what will set the Sierra Songbird

apart." Edward stroked his chin with long elegant fingers. "Yellow. Lots of yellow, like sunlight and the meadowlark's breast. Surely your fancy dressmaker can create a costume such as I've described.

"We're also not going to let some music professor turn Ellie into an opera singer. Her charm is in who she is. A few lessons in proper breathing will be all she needs." A gleam brightened his eyes. "Ellie, do you play guitar? Do you know some old ballads?"

Ellie blinked. *What on earth . . . ?* "One of our Mexican workers taught me to play the guitar, and I know dozens of ballads. I've even written a few."

Edward crossed his arms and donned a satisfied smile. "Good! I'll usually accompany you on the piano, but a guitar will be perfect for some of your songs."

Mrs. Stanhope clapped her gloved hands. For the first time, Ellie saw the older woman show genuine excitement and delight. "You're getting back to your music, Edward? I am so happy."

Ellie caught a glimpse beneath Mrs. Stanhope's outward surface. A true mother's heart beat in her tightly corseted body, at least as far as Edward was concerned. The recognition went a long way toward helping

Ellie warm up to her patroness.

She sighed, wishing Mrs. Stanhope could accept Josh for who he was. Her wish gave birth to a question: What if God was leading her to San Francisco for a greater purpose than fame and fortune? A purpose even more important than ministering to others with her voice? The prayer of the thirteenth-century monk, Saint Francis of Assisi, came to mind. Ellie had written a simple guitar accompaniment and often sang the timeless words:

Lord, make me an instrument of Thy peace;
where there is hatred, let me sow love;
where there is injury, pardon;
where there is doubt, faith;
where there is despair, hope;
where there is darkness, light;
and where there is sadness, joy.

Ellie's heart filled to overflowing. *I still want to be someone, Lord,* she prayed, *but the greatest gift I could ever bring to Joshua would be reconciliation with his family. Help me sow seeds that You may cause to grow.*

Mrs. Stanhope's voice grated into Ellie's prayer. "One thing. Don't worry about expenses. As your sponsor, I am happy to take care of your needs."

Ellie raised her chin, feeling a red tide sweep into her face. "Thank you, Mrs. Stanhope, but that won't be necessary. Matt and Seth gave me ample funds to carry me until I can begin to earn my own way."

"That will be sooner than you think," Edward promised. "We'll start by having you sing at Bayview Christian."

Josh's church. Ellie's mouth went dry. How could she sing to a congregation she suspected was waiting for their former preacher to come to his senses and return?

"Trust Me."

The words that had brought her through good times and bad stilled Ellie's trembling hands. God knew what He was doing. All she had to do was cling to His promise to never leave or forsake her. Ellie jerked her attention back to what Edward was saying.

"After that, we'll let it be known you're available for home musicales and soirees."

Dazzled by the glittering future he painted, Ellie felt her enthusiasm rise to match Edward's. Not to be outdone, his mother broke into the plans.

"I have a splendid idea!" Her face glowed. "Ellie, when you feel ready, we'll have you do a benefit concert for the Occidental Mission Home for Girls." Sadness replaced her joy. "It's too bad there has to be such a place, but thank God for Margaret Culbertson. She rescues young Chinese girls from slavery or worse."

Mrs. Stanhope set her lips in a grim line. "Desperate parents in Canton, China, sell their daughters for less than forty dollars each. Countless other girls, some only six or seven, are kidnapped and hidden aboard ships. Once they reach America, they are smuggled into San Francisco and other ports."

"How can they get past immigration?" Ellie protested. A lump came to her throat, thinking of those unfortunate girls. What she had suffered at Gus's hands was nothing compared with the girls' plight.

Edward gave a scornful laugh. "Immigration officials can be bribed. The Chinese slave traders pretend to be the girls' relatives. They carry false papers that let them smuggle the girls into Chinatown, which is only a few blocks from Nob Hill, where we live. The girls are abused and forced to work such long hours many of them don't last long. They're called the 'Children of Darkness,' and live without hope."

He clenched his fists. "I'd like to get my hands on some of those yellow slavers! They're the scourge of San Francisco. They bribe police officers to cover up for them.

Many lawyers work pro bono on the girls' behalf, but it's often impossible to obtain justice. San Francisco is a beautiful city. Many good people live in Chinatown, but it also holds opium dens, and the yellow slave trade is an indelible stain."

Ellie shuddered. What kind of place was this?

Mrs. Stanhope took up the story. "They hate Margaret Culbertson. She established the Mission Home on the very edge of Chinatown in 1874 and began raids into its dark heart. She's saved many girls from bondage. Margaret cares for their spiritual as well as their physical needs. She's one of the most courageous women I've ever met. I wish I could be more like her."

Edward patted his mother's plump hand. "You do a great deal. It takes money to keep the Occidental Mission Home going. You're tops at shaming some of our miserly leading citizens into making donations."

Her eyes twinkled. "Only because they get their names listed in the paper."

Ellie fell silent. She had never met anyone like this society matron. Mrs. Stanhope's warmhearted concern for the Chinese girls appeared at odds with her obvious desire for recognition. Perhaps she believed she'd been divinely appointed to carry out on earth the plans God made in heaven.

Edward, identical to Joshua in looks, also seemed a mass of contradictions. His bringing his mother to Madera to find a singer didn't make sense to Ellie. She pondered it while the train continued its headlong rush toward the City by the Bay. But when they left the train and boarded the ferry at Oakland, everything except her surroundings fled from Ellie's mind.

Fog hung low over San Francisco Bay, so thick she could barely see the opposite shore. Whitecaps kicked against the ferry. Ellie's nostrils twitched from the unfamiliar smell of salt. "It's not much like the Mississippi River," she mumbled, then put one hand over her mouth, thankful that the chill breeze whipped away her words. Nobody in San Francisco knew her as anyone other than Ellie Sterling. She needed to guard her tongue and keep it that way.

A mournful whistle blew. Edward helped the women off the ferry. Ellie gaped at the crowded dock and streets. Pushcarts jostled carriages. Peddlers offered their wares, screaming at the top of their lungs. Ellie shrank against Mrs. Stanhope while Edward secured a rig and said, "Nob Hill, driver." They climbed inside. The sound of horses' hooves clattering over the cobbled streets made Ellie homesick for Calico. Oh, to be back riding the range instead of in the midst of such confusion!

There was so much to see that Ellie soon forgot everything but San Francisco. The streets went up and up until it seemed they would reach the sky. A cable car clanged its way down a steep hill.

"I'll take you on the cable car someday," Edward promised.

Excitement filled Ellie. "Thank you."

They reached the top of the hill and climbed another. At last the coach stopped in front of a large, imposing house. Ellie smothered a nervous giggle. The dark brick Stanhope mansion, with its turrets, lace-curtained bay windows, fancy iron scroll-work, and balconies resembled a haughty, aging queen squatting on a throne, looking down on everyone else. Could a simple rancher's daughter ever feel at home here?

The ornate front door opened. Ellie expected a uniformed butler, but a smiling, gray-haired replica of Edward and Josh came down the steps, hands outstretched. "Welcome to our home, Miss Sterling. I'm glad you're here."

Ellie looked into Charles Stanhope's steady eyes and shyly put her hand in his. The cold knot that had parked where her heart should be ever since they boarded the ferry left. No matter what lay ahead, she'd found a friend . . . perhaps even an ally, if needed.

EIGHTEEN

From the time Ellie met Beryl Westfield, Edward's dark-haired fiancée seized every opportunity to belittle Ellie when they were alone. Yet in public, she fairly oozed sweetness and light toward "our Sierra Songbird."

"Don't pay any attention to Beryl," Edward advised Ellie one day after walking in while Beryl was making a snide comment.

Beryl glared at him and rushed out, but Edward only laughed.

"Her nose is out of joint because she pursued Josh before we got engaged. She couldn't get him. Beryl is thirty-two, five years older than we are; almost old enough to be your mother. Besides, she's also upset because I've mended my lazy ways in favor of promoting you and practicing."

Edward frowned. "Josh tries to like Beryl for my sake, but it's rough going." He clasped his hands behind his head. "Sometimes I don't like her either."

Ellie gasped. "You're going to marry someone you don't like?"

Edward had the grace to look ashamed. "I need a wife." A glint came into his gray eyes. "Too bad I didn't see you before my brother did!"

"Please don't talk like that, Edward." Ellie took a deep breath. "You mustn't marry anyone you don't love with all your heart."

"Is that the way you feel about Josh?"

Ellie sensed that a great deal hung on her answer. She could not give an evasive reply. "Yes, Edward, but it's between us and God, not you. And especially not Beryl. Now if you'll excuse me, I need to practice."

"Wait, Ellie." Edward caught at her sleeve. "Don't hold it against me for asking. Comparing a girl like you with Beryl Westfield makes a man wonder."

His comment troubled Ellie, but anxiety over her first public appearance in San Francisco left little time to worry about Edward.

At last the big day came. Ellie's knees shook as she left the Stanhope pew and started to the front of Bayview Christian Church. The distance up the richly carpeted aisle loomed longer than the miles that stretched between Madera and the Diamond S. She felt sweat trickle inside her gloved hands and smoothed down her pale yellow sleeves. Would her wobbly knees be able to carry her up the richly carpeted aisle? Would a single note come out of her parched throat? Why had she agreed to make her San Francisco debut in Joshua's church? Far better to have first sung at a home musicale.

"Trust Me."

The unspoken reminder blunted the edge of Ellie's fear. Her throat cleared. She walked to her place beside the organ, turned, and faced the congregation.

" 'It Is Well with My Soul' is my favorite hymn. Before I sing, I want you to know how the song came to be written." She paused. For a moment the richly colored stained-glass windows changed to clear glass in her mind. Sunlight streamed through them into Christ the Way Church and bathed Joshua Stanhope in its golden rays.

The image faded, but it had strengthened Ellie. She clasped her hands and said, "Horatio Spafford was a remarkable man. He, his wife, and four young daughters lived in Chicago. . . ." Ellie saw quickening interest replace the expressions of boredom and curiosity on the faces turned toward her. When she finished the story, she nodded to the organist. He struck a single note, and

Ellie's bell-like tones rang throughout the cathedral.

"When peace, like a river, attendeth my way . . ." Her voice soared with triumph, just as it had when she sang in Christ the Way. "It is well . . . with my soul. . . . It is well, it is well with my soul."

With my soul echoed back from the vaulted ceiling. Ellie looked at the Stanhope pew. Mr. Stanhope wore a look of peace that thrilled her heart. If no one else had been touched, he had. Tears coursed down Mrs. Stanhope's cheeks. Had she also been inspired by the song? Ellie's gaze turned to Edward. She saw approval in his eyes and a softening in his face. It made Edward look more like his twin than ever.

The fourth occupant of the pew looked neither exalted nor touched by the story and song. Beryl Westfield, gowned in the latest fashion, raised one haughty eyebrow and pursed her lips when Ellie walked back to the pew. Ellie's joy at the congregation's obvious approval dwindled. The enmity in the older woman's face made her shudder. She hadn't faced such dislike since the days of being taunted for being Gus's daughter. She hated the feelings Beryl stirred up. Everyone else she'd met in San Francisco had been kind. Must there always be a serpent to spoil the Garden of Eden?

Busy trying to overcome her resentment, Ellie barely heard the choir's final presentation and the benediction. She returned to reality when the Reverend Michael Yates, Josh's red-haired substitute, reached her. "Smashing, Miss Sterling. Absolutely smashing." Admiration shone in his hazel eyes. "What a team we make — you with your singing; I with my preaching!"

Edward made a choking sound. Ellie wanted to poke him. No matter how pompous Michael sounded, as a minister he deserved respect. Not wanting to encourage him, she said, "I'm glad you liked my song." Michael Yates had made his lofty ambitions clear at their first meeting. He'd also done everything but add how proud he'd be to have the Sierra Songbird help him climb the ladder to success.

Even if there were no Joshua, I couldn't care for this man, Ellie thought. *He appears far more interested in how rapidly he can rise than in being God's servant and leading souls to Christ.* How different Michael Yates was from Josh, who had walked away from the position Michael obviously coveted.

Josh crumpled the third version of a letter to Ellie and tossed it toward the big wood-

190

stove in the parsonage. He missed his target, just as he missed Ellie. She'd only been gone a few weeks, but it seemed like forever. Josh pulled the single letter she'd written to him from the pocket above his heart, smoothed out the creases, and spread the pages on his table. Worn from many readings, they threatened to fall apart. He read the words he had already memorized:

Dear Josh,

I hardly know where to start. San Francisco is beautiful, ugly, inviting, and terrifying. I am in awe of its magnificent structures but appalled at the stories I hear about the yellow slave trade. I sometimes want to flee, but the continuing belief that God has put me here for a reason prevents my turning tail and running.

Almost everyone has been incredibly kind. Your father is everything I wish mine had been. Your mother treats me like an honored guest and delights in advising me about proper dress. To my surprise, she approves of everything I brought from home. However, she has insisted on having some gowns made for more formal occasions and when I perform.

Edward is really a dear, not at all what I expected when I first met him. He's so much like you that when I'm with him, I sometimes forget he isn't you!

Josh raised his head and gazed out the window. September had waved farewell and ushered in October. Tree branches swayed in the gentle breeze. Busy squirrels searched for winter store. Peace lay over the smiling land but failed to touch Josh.

"The last thing I need is for Ellie to start thinking Edward's just like me," he muttered, cringing at the thought. "Such an idea could lead to heartbreak. If ever two persons were unequally yoked, they are Ellie and my brother."

She could be the making of Edward, a little voice mocked. *Beryl Westfield is a self-confessed infidel. Ellie is the finest example of Christian womanhood. Beryl attracts with her sophistication. Ellie appeals because of her lack of sophistication.*

Josh grunted. "Lord, if I gave up Ellie, which I'm not going to do, there's no guarantee Edward would change permanently, even if he won her."

The little voice remained mercifully silent, so Josh returned to the letter:

I never dreamed how different San Francisco could be from the Diamond S. Edward has taken me to ride the cable cars and to Golden Gate Park, always suitably chaperoned, of course. We ride there, but it's nothing like being on Calico. I long to be on her back and riding with the wind in my face.

The Pacific Ocean took my breath away. So did walking along the Embarcadero with its salty, fishy smell. Two of my favorite places are the Conservatory in Golden Gate Park and the Palace Hotel. Edward says I may someday be able to sing there, but not until I'm better known. I couldn't believe it when the carriage we were in drove right into the Grand Court. Forgive me for gushing about things you know so well. They're all new and strange to me.

Ellie went on to describe her first solo at Bayview Christian and added:

When I sang "It Is Well with My Soul," I didn't expect the congregation here to react the same as those at Christ the Way. But they did. Your mother and Edward say it must become my signature song. No matter where or what else I sing, I'm to save the story and song for the end of the program. Your father agrees. He says nothing else can reach people like the song. I'm glad. Each time I sing it, I think of you telling the story of it being ripped from the depths of a hurting heart. It makes me homesick, but it also makes me proud to pass the story on. My prayer is that it may touch lives the way it touched mine.

By the way, Reverend Michael Yates approves of me. He says we make a great team because of my singing and his preaching. The first time he said it, I wanted to laugh. Edward nearly disgraced himself by choking. You should have seen the look Beryl gave him.

Josh slammed his fist on the table. "This is the last straw. I not only have to worry about Edward, but this Yates clown is obviously on Ellie's trail, too. So he thinks they make a great team. Not if I have anything to say about it. Yates has another think coming." Josh returned to the letter once more:

I miss everyone and long for the time when God leads me back to Madera.

Ellie

Josh left the pages on the table and sought

the silence of his church. He knelt before the altar and bowed his head. *Lord, bring Ellie home to me,* his heart cried. *I need her so much.* Fear of losing her and the weight of recent events fell heavily on Josh's bent shoulders. Slowly but surely, Luther Talbot and his cohorts were making inroads on Josh's acceptance.

"Lord, my hopes for happiness here seem short lived," he prayed. "All I want is to find and serve those who need You. Now I'm facing a mountain of resistance. Luther, the board, and many of the congregation frown on my desire to spend time outside the church walls. They continually remind me I was hired to minister to the flock already securely in the fold, not go chasing after wild sheepherders and cowhands."

Josh stopped his prayer long enough to mutter, "I can't believe Luther's latest complaint." He mimicked the board chairman's accusing voice. " 'You've been here since June, Reverend. What good has come of all your gallivanting around? Only one of those lost sheep you've been so eager to bring to the Lord has come to the altar.' "

Josh chuckled. "I bit my tongue to keep from telling Luther that one soul saved in the time I've been here isn't so bad. Noah preached for 120 years and only succeeded in saving eight people from the flood, including himself."

Laughter gave way to depression and doubt. "Was I wrong in thinking Madera is where You want me to serve? And that Ellie is the woman You've chosen to be my wife — even though Edward can make her San Francisco's Sierra Songbird?"

Hours later Josh returned to his home with his concerns unresolved. "Well Lord," he prayed as he lay in bed watching the brilliant stars filling the sky outside his open window, "Your answers are *yes, no,* and *wait.* This time it must be *wait.*"

An owl hooted from the spreading oak tree. A coyote yapped for its mate in the distance. Its mournful wail sounded as lonely as Josh felt. Yet the crooning of the crisp, early October night wind soothed the troubled young preacher, and at last he slept.

NINETEEN

Ellie sat by the window of her bedroom in the Stanhope mansion. If only the sun would break through the heavy gray fog blanket that obscured the usually magnificent view! Thankful that for once she had a few minutes to herself, she breathed a sigh of relief. Ever since she'd arrived in the city, life had galloped at a pace that sometimes left her disoriented. After her first solo at Bayview Christian, she'd been deluged with invitations to sing, thanks to an enterprising reporter who'd been in church that Sunday. He'd helped launch her whirlwind rise to fame with a glowing review of her solo in the *San Francisco Chronicle.* Then he periodically added tidbits guaranteed to pique the interest of persons looking for something new and worthwhile.

A demanding knock sounded on Ellie's door. Before she could respond, it slammed open. Beryl Westfield, face contorted with fury, rushed in. "You innocent-faced minx! Have you seen this?"

The discordant voice jerked Ellie from her solitude. She peered at Beryl. Impeccably dressed as usual, the hatred in Beryl's black eyes made Ellie cringe. Beryl flung a copy of the *Chronicle* at her and demanded, "Read that!"

Ellie caught the paper before it struck her in the face. She glanced down. Her image stared back at her from beside the bold headline: SIERRA SONGBIRD SOARS.

"What's wrong?" Ellie faltered. "It's just an article."

"Just an article?" Beryl raved, hands clenched into fists. She took a menacing step toward Ellie. "Read the whole thing!"

Ellie blinked. Had Beryl gone crazy, to come tearing in, raging like this?

"Read it!"

Ellie shrank from the older woman, who stood watching her like an avenging angel. No, more like someone under Satan's control. Beryl evidently wouldn't leave until she got what she'd come for. Ellie read the headline again, then the article:

SIERRA SONGBIRD SOARS

San Franciscans are taking note of a

newcomer to our fair city. Miss Ellianna Sterling first captivated the congregation (and this reporter) at Bayview Christian Church with her remarkable voice. Miss Sterling is the protégée of Mrs. Charles Stanhope, well-known benefactress and champion of the downtrodden.

Sought after for soirees and musicales by San Francisco's finest, the Sierra Songbird, as she is known, is winning both high praise and our hearts. Her modest dress, simple ballads — including some she has written — and her hymns have shaken San Francisco. Sterling's simplicity and lack of vanity impress even the most jaded music lovers. She prefaces the heartfelt rendition of her signature song, "It Is Well with My Soul," with the story of how it came to be written. Few of us remain dry-eyed when confronted by the author's unwavering faith.

Neither can we resist the expression on the songbird's face when she sings, " 'Even so, it is well with my soul.' " It bears mute but compelling testimony: Whatever others choose to believe, it truly is well with Ellianna Sterling's soul.

The Sierra Songbird is often accompanied by Edward Stanhope, whose proficiency at the piano has until now been unsuspected. The dark-haired man and the yellow-gowned singer make a striking couple. One cannot help wondering if there would be wedding bells as well as church bells in their future were it not for Edward's engagement to Miss Beryl Westfield.

Tickets are now being offered at premium prices for a concert benefiting Mrs. Stanhope's favorite charity, The Occidental Mission Home for Girls. It is one event this reporter plans to cover, and not just to get a story.

Ellie let the paper slip through her fingers to the rich Oriental rug. She had run the gamut of emotions while reading it. Joy. Excitement. Gratitude for the reporter's kind words about her singing. The thrill of knowing God was using her to touch lives. But the comment about a wedding and church bells destroyed Ellie's pleasure and filled her with disgust. She jumped from her chair and faced Beryl.

"Why did the reporter have to spoil all the nice things he said by hinting at a romance between Edward and me?" she cried. "It isn't true, Miss Westfield. Edward is my friend, nothing more."

Beryl's eyes narrowed into cat's eyes. "If

that's true, then why has he been making me a laughingstock by escorting you all over the city?"

"We always have a chaperone," Ellie told her. "Maria or one of the other maids accompanies us."

Beryl brushed her comment aside. "Even if I believed you, which I don't, it doesn't matter. My friends mock me because Edward is never available when I want him." She drew herself up to her full height and glowered down at Ellie. "Edward has also begun to hint that perhaps we aren't suited for one another. I pleased him well enough until you came." Venom dripped from every word.

Snippets of a conversation from weeks earlier popped into Ellie's mind:

"Sometimes I don't like her myself."

"You're going to marry someone you don't like?"

"I need a wife."

"You mustn't marry anyone you don't love with all your heart."

"Comparing a girl like you with Beryl Westfield makes a man wonder."

"Well?" Beryl's harsh voice sent the memory flying, but not before Ellie's heart leaped. She'd come to like Edward — first because he reminded her of Josh, then for his dedication to helping her succeed. If he was having second thoughts about joining his life with Beryl, it was all to the good.

Ellie carefully hid her elation at the thought. "I have told you the truth, Miss Westfield. I have nothing more to say. Now will you please leave my room?"

Beryl's face went chalk white. She raised one hand as if to strike. Then she said, "Watch your step. To quote that Bible you so piously hide behind while trying to worm your way in where you don't belong, 'Pride goeth before a fall.' "

"It's actually 'Pride goeth before destruction, and an haughty spirit before a fall,' " Ellie told her.

The unwelcome guest gave Ellie another scorching look and marched out. Shaken, Ellie sank back into her chair. "Lord, what am I doing here?"

"Trust Me."

Ellie buried her face in her hands and cried out, "I do trust You, but it's hard! I haven't done anything to deserve such treatment."

"Neither did My Son."

The silent reminder poured healing into Ellie's hurting heart. She continued to sit by the window and look out into the gray day, taking stock of her present life. At times, her St. Louis childhood seemed distant and unreal. Even her years on the Diamond S were gradually losing their luster when compared with the glory of rising from obscurity to being sought after. Only her love for her family and Joshua remained constant.

"I'll enjoy it while it lasts," she vowed. "Someday Joshua and I will be reunited. In the meantime, I'm saving money in case Tim needs it. Also, when the time comes, I won't have to go to Joshua like a penniless beggar girl."

Joy welled into Ellie's throat and rippled out. "I'm also helping Josh, even though he doesn't know it. Lord, thank You for making Mr. Stanhope so understanding. When I told him I wanted to send my tithe to Christ the Way Church anonymously he arranged it. I'm sure he never said a word to Mrs. Stanhope or Edward or they would have asked why I'd do such a thing."

The solemn chime of a clock put an end to Ellie's rejoicing. She'd be late for her music lesson if she didn't hurry. She washed her hands and face, tidied her shining hair, and ran downstairs, carrying her hooded cloak. To her dismay, Beryl stood with

Edward in the great hall. Her rigid stance showed she still burned with anger.

Edward looked up. "Beryl reminded me of an important engagement this afternoon, Ellie. She's helping Mother with the arrangements for the benefit concert, and of course they need my expert advice. We'll drop you off on the way, but I don't know how long it will take. I've told our carriage driver to pick you up after your lesson. Sorry."

"There's no need to be sorry." Ellie slipped into her cloak and followed them out to the carriage. She climbed in, being careful to leave the place beside Edward for Beryl. When they reached her music teacher's studio, she stepped down and said, "Be careful. It looks like the fog is getting worse."

"We will. I'll see you at home later," Edward called as they trotted away.

Ellie hurried inside, glad to get out of the penetrating moisture that threatened to soak through her heavy cloak. She greeted her teacher and the lesson began. Partway through, however, a message came. Her instructor read it and blanched.

"I have to leave, Miss Sterling. A dear friend has taken ill and needs me."

"It's all right," Ellie assured him. "I can

wait here. The Stanhope carriage will come for me at the regular time."

He looked dubious but apologized again and left.

Ellie busied herself with straightening piles of music that lay askew, but soon tired of the task. Why stay in this empty studio when it was less than a mile from home? She had time to walk and be there long before the driver left to pick her up.

Once outside, she hesitated. "Don't be foolish," she told herself. "You can't get lost between here and Nob Hill." Ellie pulled the hood of her cloak over her hair, clutched its voluminous folds around her body against the encroaching cold, and confidently started up the street.

All too soon, the fog thickened. It changed to a drizzle. Its eerie *drip-drip* added to the chilling atmosphere. Ellie increased her pace, anxious to get out of the murk that swallowed up the street signs. A few blocks farther on, she murmured, "Better to wait in the studio than in this pea soup." She shivered with cold and turned to retrace her steps. Her foot slipped on a pebble. Ellie tried to regain her balance, but fell, hitting her head on the cobblestone street.

Dizzy and disoriented, Ellie staggered to her feet and rubbed her throbbing head.

She tried to remember whether she should be walking up the hill or down. Did it really matter? If she kept walking, she'd get somewhere. Yet each uncertain step brought new fear. Where *was* she?

She rounded a corner. Dim lights flickered through the fog curtain. Thank goodness! Light meant help lay just ahead. Ellie broke into a run. More lights appeared, still faint, but enough to show alleys on both sides of the street. Stairs led to second and third stories. Dark, shadowy forms huddled in gaping doorways. Muffled voices speaking a language Ellie didn't understand floated through the fog.

She stopped short and peered through the gloom at a brightly colored banner with strange black symbols. Her heart hammered with fear. Confused by the fog, she had stumbled into Chinatown — the last place she should be alone with night coming on.

Yellow slave traders. The scourge of San Francisco. Opium dens. Children of Darkness. Many good people in Chinatown, but a stain on the city.

Ellie's stomach lurched. She turned to flee, but a heavy hand caught her by the shoulder. A disembodied voice gloated, "I've got you now. 'Tis about time."

Ellie tried to wrench free. She could not.

She tried to scream. Only a squeak came out of her constricted throat, so muffled by the fog no one except her captor would ever hear her. *Dear God, why didn't I stay at the studio where I belonged?*

TWENTY

The grip on Ellie's shoulder tightened. The fog-hoarsened voice ordered, "Don't try to fly, little birdie. You and your kind are for belongin' in the paddy wagon, not on the streets."

Your kind? Paddy wagon? What did he mean? Ellie twisted around and peered into her captor's face. She sagged with relief. Enough light shone on brass buttons marching down the burly figure's chest to identify him. A policeman. The biggest, most forbidding policeman she'd ever seen. Surely he'd get her out of her predicament and back to the Stanhopes!

A none-too-gentle shake brought doubt hard on the heels of Ellie's relief. "Is it the cat's got your tongue?"

Ellie's mind churned. Icy fear licked at her veins. Her body shook. What if this policeman with the iron grip was a devil in disguise? One of the police officers the

Chinese smugglers bribed to wink at their dark deeds? Terror turned Ellie legs to overcooked spaghetti. Only the firm hold on her shoulder kept her from tumbling to the wet cobblestone street.

The policeman leaned down until his broad, scowling face was level with Ellie's. He gave a muffled exclamation and released her, but caught her with both hands when she stumbled and nearly fell. "Miss Sterling? Faith and mercy, why are you for bein' in such a place?"

The rich Irish voice dispelled fear, but Ellie tried twice before she could give a disjointed explanation. "The fog. I lost my way. Thank God you're here!"

"I'll also be for thankin' God. Beggin' your pardon, but with the hood over your head and you bein' out on such a night I mistook you for . . . uh —" He broke off.

Ellie wrinkled her forehead. "How did you recognize me?"

The policeman's brogue deepened. "Thanks to the *Chronicle,* everyone's for knowin' the Sierra Songbird. Come along, colleen. You're safe with Clancy. I'll for shure be havin' you home shortly."

Ellie had to run to keep up with her rescuer's long strides that gobbled up the distance between Chinatown and Nob Hill.

When Clancy delivered her to the Stanhope mansion, she impulsively said, "I didn't know there were Irish guardian angels, but you were mine tonight."

Clancy's laugh rang out, warming Ellie in spite of the chill night. "I've niver been called an angel before, but I'm glad 'twas me who found you." He scowled and became the grim policeman who had frightened her. "Don't you be for runnin' around alone at night, *mavourneen.* There are spalpeens in this city who would delight in clipping our songbird's wings, cagin' her, and holdin' her for ransom."

Ellie shuddered at his warning. "I promise." She held out her hand, and Clancy engulfed it in his. "Will you come in?" she invited when the door swung open and Edward stepped out. She could see Mr. and Mrs. Stanhope standing in the hall behind him.

Clancy shook his head. "I'm on duty." He raised his voice and called, "She's for bein' safe," then respectfully touched his hat and vanished into the fog.

"Ellie? Where have you been? Why was that policeman with you?" Edward took her arm and led her into the hall. The heavy door closed behind them. Light from the chandelier in the great hall streamed down, a welcome contrast to the dark, miserable night lurking outside the mansion. It showed the worry lines etched in the three faces turned toward her.

Suddenly aware of her disheveled appearance, Ellie sensed her nerves starting to unravel. If she related the Chinatown incident now she'd be forced to run the gauntlet of horrified questions and relive her terror. She couldn't handle it. Ellie bit her lips to hide their trembling. "My instructor had to leave early. I started to walk home but lost my way. A policeman found me and brought me home. Please excuse me. I need a hot bath and dry clothes." She slid out of her sodden cloak and handed it to Maria, who had come into the hall with a concerned look on her pretty face.

"Go draw a bath for Miss Ellie," Mrs. Stanhope told the maid.

"Si." Maria disappeared with the cloak. By the time Ellie slowly trudged upstairs, the Mexican girl had already poured a generous amount of fragrant bath salts in the claw-footed tub and stood waiting to take away Ellie's wet clothing when she shed it.

"Gracias," Ellie told her.

Maria's eyes sparkled with fun. "Senorita, you look more like a robin with its feathers ruffled from a windstorm than our song-bird!"

"I feel that way, too." Ellie yawned.

"Do not fall asleep in the bath," Maria warned. "Senora Stanhope says dinner will not be served until you come. Senor Marvin Stanhope is to be a guest."

She whisked away, leaving Ellie to luxuriate in the scented water.

Ellie felt tempted to ask for dinner in her room but reconsidered. Ever since arriving in San Francisco, she'd been eager to meet Charles's brother — who defied Stanhope expectations by serving down-and-outs at his Rescue Mission.

Ellie finished her bath and towel-dried her hair until it curled under against the nape of her neck. She slipped into the pale blue dimity dress Maria had laid out for her and fastened the ribbons on her flat slippers. Her heart quickened to double time. What would the man Joshua admired so deeply think of her? Had Josh mentioned her to his uncle? If so, would the street missionary find her worthy of his beloved nephew?

One look into Marvin Stanhope's keen gray eyes set Ellie's doubts at rest. He bore a strong resemblance to the other Stanhope men. Ellie immediately felt at home with him and delighted when placed beside him at the glittering dining room table. He plied her with questions about Joshua.

Ellie clasped her hands and spoke more freely than she had felt comfortable doing except to Josh's father. She tingled with excitement. "He is wonderful," she said, aware of Marvin's keen interest and the way Mrs. Stanhope and Edward leaned forward to hear. "If it hadn't been for Joshua, a mountain lion would have killed my brother, Tim."

Mrs. Stanhope's silver fork crashed to her fine china plate. Her face paled, and she stared at Ellie. "A mountain lion! Why haven't you told me about that?"

Ellie wished she had bitten her tongue instead of blurting out the news in an attempt to show how splendid Joshua was. "I–I'm sorry. I knew it would worry you."

Mrs. Stanhope's voice rose a full octave. "What happened?"

"A rifle shot wounded the lion. It came toward Tim and Joshua. Tim's rifle misfired and knocked the lion down. The rifle landed at Josh's feet. He grabbed it and knocked the beast senseless. The other men came and killed it."

Mrs. Stanhope raised a handkerchief to her lips with trembling hands. "I knew no good would come of my son going to Madera." She whirled toward her brother-in-law. "This wouldn't have happened if you hadn't lured Joshua to your mission when he was only a boy."

"Settle down, Mother. Uncle Marvin didn't send Josh to Madera. God did." Edward spoke gently, and his father nodded in agreement.

Edward's unexpected defense of his brother caught Ellie by surprise. She wouldn't have expected him to admit that God was responsible for Joshua's choice. Was the prodigal twin softening toward spiritual things? *Please, Lord, let it be so. I can hardly wait to write and tell Josh what Edward said.*

Some of the color returned to Mrs. Stanhope's face. She beckoned to Maria, who gaped in the background. "You may serve dessert now."

When the maid left the room, Ellie said, "You can all be proud of Joshua. He's doing a great deal of good under difficult circumstances."

Mrs. Stanhope bridled. "Why should my son be experiencing difficult circumstances after all he gave up here?"

For the second time, Ellie regretted speaking before weighing her words as she'd been doing since coming to San Francisco. Her heart sank. "Some of the board members disagree with his methods."

Edward chortled. "That's nothing new. I remember hearing of trouble in the ranks of Bayview Christian a time or two over Josh's . . . uh . . . sometimes unorthodox means of getting his message across." Not giving his mother a chance to answer, he immediately turned back to his uncle. "How are things at the mission?"

Ellie gave a secret sigh of relief and drank in every word of their guest's reply. But when he turned to her and said, "Miss Sterling, would you consider coming to the Rescue Mission and singing?" the hush that fell over the diners left her paralyzed. Edward's mouth fell open. His father's eyes twinkled. And Mrs. Stanhope looked as if she'd been turned to stone. Why didn't someone say something to break the shocked silence?

Ellie thought of her Chinatown ordeal. The Rescue Mission was located in one of the worst parts of San Francisco. Panic sent perspiration crawling down Ellie's body. How could she deliberately go to a place so filled with danger and sin? Something terrible might happen to her.

"Trust Me."

Ellie swallowed hard and took a deep,

unsteady breath. When she released it and spoke, her words came out in a whisper. "I will go."

"No!" Edward leaped to his feet, overturning his chair. It crashed to the costly carpet with a muffled *thud*. Fury mottled his face. "Are you insane? I won't hear of it. It isn't safe." He glared at his uncle. "How dare you make such a suggestion? Unspeakable things happen down there."

His uncle softly replied, "Psalm 118 says, 'The Lord is on my side; I will not fear: what can man do unto me?' Ellie will be perfectly safe. You can deliver her in a closed carriage with a bodyguard if you wish. Once inside the mission, every man there will fight to defend her should the need arise, which it won't." The zeal in the man's eyes made him look more like Joshua than ever. "Edward, Letitia, think. Who needs the Sierra Songbird more? Those who already know the way, the truth, and the life? Or the lost sheep?"

A glorious light crept into Charles Stanhope's face. "I will personally take Ellie to the mission." He raised a commanding hand when his wife started to protest. "The subject is closed. Marvin is right. Ellie can do more good with her songs and stories down there than we may ever know." He smiled at Maria, who had brought a silver tray holding frozen pudding to the table. "I suggest we finish our dinner and prevail on our songbird to favor us with a number."

To Ellie's surprise, Mrs. Stanhope and Edward subsided, but the storm clouds hanging heavy in their faces showed they didn't consider the matter settled. Ellie did. She had given her word.

Weary beyond belief from the day's events, Ellie found herself wound tightly after their guest left. Her brain raced like a caged squirrel. *Beryl. The* Chronicle *article. Chinatown. Marvin Stanhope's plea.* Knowing she would not sleep until she rid herself of the memories, Ellie snatched writing materials and wrote a letter to Tim, a letter in which she poured out all her wrought-up feelings.

At last she slept. The next morning, the hastily written missive began its journey to the Diamond S.

TWENTY-ONE

A few days later, Edward stalked into the breakfast room where Ellie was having a solitary meal. He flung a copy of the *San Francisco Chronicle* on the table in front of Ellie. "Read this," he thundered. "How did that meddlesome reporter get wind of it?"

Ellie glanced down:

SIERRA SONGBIRD TO PERFORM AT RESCUE MISSION

The latest news about Ellianna Sterling, who has captured the hearts of San Franciscans with her incredible voice and sweet personality, is indeed shocking. Miss Sterling plans to visit one of the meanest streets in our city and sing at the Rescue Mission. The mission, which offers 'soup, soap, and salvation,' is operated by Marvin Stanhope, long considered eccentric for turning his back on society in favor of a life of service.

An unnamed source confirms that what began as a rumor is now fact. When asked why she would even consider such an outrageous venture the Sierra Songbird replied, "Jesus went to the lost sheep. Should I do less?"

This reporter is torn between applauding the young lady's courage and dashing to her rescue like a knight in the days of old.

"How can the reporter know this?" Ellie cried. "Who is his unnamed source?" She fixed an accusing stare on Edward. "The only person I told how I felt was you!"

The anger in Edward's face changed to chagrin. He clutched his head in both hands. "I was so upset about your going to the mission that I blurted it out to Beryl. Ellie, I am so sorry."

Appetite gone, Ellie pushed back from the table and slumped in her chair. "This must be her revenge for the speculation about us."

Edward dropped into a chair next to her. "It's more than speculation, Ellie. I've broken with Beryl for good. She blames you." A corner of his mouth lifted in a lopsided smile. "It really is your fault, you know. No man in his right mind would marry a woman like Beryl when there are girls like you in the world."

"Stop." She raised her hands in mute appeal. "You know how I feel about Joshua."

"Don't worry about it." Edward cocked one eyebrow and became his usual fun-loving self. "If good ol' Josh were anyone but my twin, I'd fall in love with you. He is, and I won't." A scowl replaced Edward's teasing expression. He folded his arms across his chest and added, "I can't say the same for the present pastor of Bayview Christian. Watch your step, Miss Sterling, or you'll be Mrs. Michael Yates in spite of yourself. He's determined to get to the top. What better way to achieve success than with the Sierra Songbird as his wife?"

Ellie didn't say so, but Edward's evaluation matched her opinion of Michael. He never lost an opportunity to praise her and send languishing looks her way. Suddenly lighthearted by Edward's promise not to fall in love with her, she brushed aside the thought of Michael, clasped her hands, and gave a mock sigh. "Oh, to be loved for myself alone, not just to help fulfill someone's ambitions."

Edward twirled an imaginary mustache in the best stage villain tradition. "Beware, my pretty. Greed and ambition lurk in the hearts of men."

Ellie laughed at his nonsense. "Are we practicing this morning as usual?"

Edward abandoned his dastardly role. "Of course. You want to sing your best for the derelicts as well as for society — unless I can talk you out of going to the mission."

"You can't."

"I know. You, young lady, are a very determined person."

A few hours later, Ellie had need of every ounce of determination she could muster. Maria appeared at her open door. Her dark eyes sparkled. "You have a visitor. Senor Yates is waiting in the library. Senora Stanhope says you are to come at once."

"Bother!" Ellie laid down her Bible. "Just when I thought I'd have time to study."

The Mexican girl came closer. "You read about *Jesús*, si?"

"Si." Ellie smiled at her. "Jesus is my best Friend."

Maria touched the silver cross she wore. "I love Jesús, too. But I think Senor Yates wants to be more than a best friend." She clapped one hand over her mouth and left before Ellie could reply.

Unnerved by Maria's comment, Ellie reluctantly went down the curving stairway. Singing at Bayview Christian meant working closely with the Reverend Michael Yates. She'd known for some time he saw her as a means to an end, and it troubled her. If he'd come to declare his intentions to marry her, how could she turn him down without incurring his wrath? She entered the room lined with rare editions and fine paintings and chose a chair rather than the settee in order to distance herself from her uninvited guest.

After inquiring after Ellie's health as if she were an invalid, the young minister said, "Miss Ellie, I've come to lay my heart at your feet and beg for your hand in marriage. I need a wife." He gave her an ardent look. "In all my many travels I've found no one so eminently suitable as you."

Ellie covered a giggle with a cough. The first part of his proposal sounded like it had been lifted from an advice to the lovelorn article in the *Chronicle*. Ellie had started to read THREE EASY WAYS TO ASK A LADY TO MARRY YOU, but had been interrupted after the first suggestion: "Be bold."

I wonder what the other two ideas were. Ellie stifled another giggle. *Michael must not have read them either. Telling me he's found no one else suitable surely couldn't be part of the article.*

Michael paced the room, and his smooth

voice painted their future in eloquent, glowing terms. Face aflame with zeal and self-importance, he ended by saying, "Think of it, Miss Ellie. There's no limit to what we can do together. We'll lead multitudes to Christ. First we conquer San Francisco, then the nation. I'll go down in history as one of the greatest preachers of all times." He placed one hand over his heart. "And you will be my inspiration."

Although disgusted by his conceit, the prospect of the glorious future he promised sliced through Ellie's common sense. What an opportunity to show those persecutors who had made her feel like Job's grand-daughter!

As if sensing her response, Michael knelt at Ellie's side and captured her hands. His hazel eyes gleamed. "I'm determined to marry you. Help me fulfill my dreams."

Ellie came to earth with a dull *thud*. His dreams? What about hers? Even if she loved Michael, which she didn't, as his wife she'd never be more than a small star hitched to a flaming comet. "I don't love you."

He squeezed her hands. "You will." Confidence rang in every word.

It sounded to Ellie like a veiled threat. She remembered Edward's warning: *Watch your step . . . or you'll be Mrs. Michael Yates in spite of yourself.* How could she convince him otherwise?

Tell him who your real father is, a little voice replied. *If Michael knew your background, he'd thank his lucky stars for saving him. Of course, telling him would also bring your house built on sand crashing down around you and end your career.*

Never! She snatched her hands free and exclaimed, "Michael, I love another man."

He leaped up and glared down at her, face redder than his hair. "Stanhope, I presume. Why have you been leading me on and making me think —"

Ellie shot out of her chair and planted her hands on her hips. She wanted to scream but kept her voice low. "Reverend Yates, I've never led you on. You're the one who has obviously planned a future and worked me in like the missing piece of a puzzle. I don't fit into your life. I never will."

A vein throbbed in Michael's throat. He gave an unpleasant laugh. "Edward Stanhope has nothing to offer you but a tarnished reputation. When you come to your senses you'll be knocking on my door, begging me to marry you. Just don't count on my still being available." He stomped out, leaving Ellie cold and shaken.

"Edward?" she whispered. "Reverend

Yates thinks I'm in love with Edward." Unwilling to meet anyone until she could control herself, Ellie took refuge in her room. She couldn't set Michael straight without betraying Joshua. Edward knew she loved his twin. His parents did not. Ellie shivered. Would Michael add to the speculation already running rampant about her and Edward? What if it reached Joshua? The idea appalled her.

Ellie clenched and unclenched her hands in an effort to relax. "As long as Reverend Yates believes I may come running to him, he will hold his tongue," she told herself. "I should be safe from unfounded rumors — at least for now — because of his pride."

Tired of the whole mess, Ellie flung herself on her bed. Why must life be so complicated? If again given the choice between the Diamond S and San Francisco, which road would she take? There, she'd been Ellie Sterling, adopted daughter of Matt and Sarah. Here, the city lay at her slippered feet.

Honesty compelled her to confess, "Lord, I don't know. I miss Josh and Tim and home, but . . ."

Ellie fell into a troubled sleep with her questions unanswered. Hours later, she awakened from a jumbled dream crying out,

"What would San Francisco say if they knew me as Ellie Stoddard, not Ellie Sterling?"

Late one afternoon, drumming hoofbeats jerked Josh from the sermon he'd been preparing. A clear voice shouted, "Whoa, Blue!"

Josh sprang out of his chair and into the yard.

Tim Sterling shot out of the saddle, eyes blazing. "Ellie's gotta come home. She's being ruined and coulda got herself killed." He coughed and slapped dust from his pants. "Gimme some water. I'm dry as a bone."

Dread filled Josh's soul. "Come in before someone hears you." Once inside, he brought a tall glass of water and motioned for Tim to sit down. "What's this all about?"

Tim drained the glass and dropped into a chair, breathing hard. He tossed Josh a wrinkled letter. "See for yourself."

Josh unfolded the pages and silently began reading:

Dear Tim,

I hardly know where to begin. San Francisco is both breathtaking and terrible. Thanks to the Stanhopes and a reporter who heard me sing, I've been praised until I'm in danger of being spoiled. Sometimes I wonder why I'm here, but most of the time I'm too busy to think clearly. Besides, I know God wants me here.

I don't like being talked about, but I'm learning to accept it. Being the target of gossip isn't new to me, and it's the price required for rising to the top, as I'm determined to do.

Josh stopped reading. Disappointment swept through him. "I hate hearing Ellie talk like that. It sounds as if she's already starting to change."

"Yeah." Tim slumped in his chair and stuck his lower lip out. "I'd like to yank her back here where she belongs."

"So would I." Josh returned to the letter:

My life is mountaintops and valleys. Edward has been wonderful, but his fiancée doesn't like me. She's the only one who makes me feel like an intruder. Definitely a valley experience!

I had an adventure late this afternoon. I decided to walk from the music studio to the Stanhopes. I got turned around in the fog and ended up in Chinatown.

"Chinatown!" Josh felt himself pale. The writing blurred. The letter fell to his lap.

Tim hurtled from his chair and paced the floor. "If a policeman hadn't found her, who knows what would've happened? That's not all," he raved. "She's gonna go sing at your uncle's Rescue Mission. Red Fallon told me what it's like down there." Worry lines added years to his face. "I don't care if your dad and brother are going with her. Why don't you tell Ellie to get back here where she belongs?"

Josh spread his hands helplessly. "I can't do that, Tim. No one can but God."

Tim turned his back on Josh and said in a muffled voice, "I know, but He'd better hurry up before something awful happens to her."

Josh got up and gave Tim's shoulder a comforting pat. "God knows best, even when we don't understand. I get the feeling Ellie thinks San Francisco is the pot of gold at the end of the rainbow."

"More like fool's gold." Tim whirled toward Josh. "Why don't you go find out what's happening? Don't tell Ellie you're coming. Just show up." He didn't wait for a reply, but glanced out the door. "It's getting late. I gotta go. Don't forget what I said."

Josh watched his young friend vault to

Blue's saddle and ride off in the threatening dusk. Forget? As if he could. Tim's startling suggestion and the news about Ellie had triggered temptation. Why not chuck his job, go to San Francisco, and fight the brother Ellie found "wonderful" for her love?

"Sorry, Lord," he mumbled. But when morning followed a sleepless night, Josh had reached a decision. His trial period would be over in a few weeks. He'd give Luther Talbot and his whiners an ultimatum: Either Preacher Josh would be free to minister outside the building as well as inside, or they could get themselves another man. And the day his six months ended, Josh would catch the first train west and leave his future in God's hands.

TWENTY-TWO

A glorious rainbow hung over San Francisco on the morning of the day Ellie was to sing at Marvin Stanhope's mission. Ellie drank in the sight from her bedroom window. She needed to talk with Mrs. Stanhope, but couldn't tear herself away until the last shimmering remnant disappeared.

Ellie found Mrs. Stanhope reading in the library. The girl had long since discovered the way to her sponsor's heart was to ask for advice, so she went right to the point. "I know you don't approve of my going to the Rescue Mission, but I need your help."

Mrs. Stanhope sighed. "I don't approve, but Charles assures me you won't be in any danger. I must admit that good has come from the *Chronicle* article about your singing there. Tickets for our Occidental Mission Home for Girls benefit concert are sold out. There's also a long waiting list." Her blue eyes gleamed with excitement.

Ellie remembered her experience in Chinatown and shuddered. "I'd sing my heart out to help Margaret Culbertson's work."

"Good for you!" The approval in the older woman's voice thrilled Ellie. In the weeks she'd been in San Francisco, her patroness had gone from pride in her protégée to obvious fondness. After the first concert, she'd made Ellie feel like a daughter of the house. Ellie felt red flags fly in her hot cheeks. God willing, perhaps one day Mrs. Stanhope would be willing to accept her as Josh's wife.

"What is it you need?" Mrs. Stanhope inquired.

Ellie put aside her daydreams. "I need advice on how to dress tonight. Should I wear a simple calico? I don't want to be so dressed up the men will be uncomfortable."

Mrs. Stanhope fitted her well-manicured fingers together. "Let me think." She wrinkled her forehead. "You're right in not wanting to cause embarrassment. It isn't the socially acceptable thing to do."

Ellie suppressed a grin. Leave it to Mrs. Stanhope to think of that.

"On the other hand, I'm sure the . . . uh . . . residents at the mission have seen your picture in the *Chronicle*. If you dress too plainly, the men may think you feel they aren't worthy of fine clothes."

"I hadn't thought of that." Ellie looked at her sponsor with respect. It seemed out of character, yet why should it? Autocratic and determined to have her own way, Mrs. Stanhope had a warm heart, as evidenced by her concern for the young Chinese girls in the city.

"Let's go look over your wardrobe."

"All right." Ellie trotted up the stairs after Mrs. Stanhope.

One by one, Ellie's lovely gowns were inspected. "Wear this new white muslin," Mrs. Stanhope advised. "It's pretty but simple. Wear a yellow sash, and I'll order a corsage of yellow roses."

A rush of admiration for her contradictory benefactress filled Ellie. "I don't suppose you would want to come with us," she blurted out.

"I? Go to the Rescue Mission? I wouldn't be caught —" She broke off.

Ellie saw an unexpected struggle between dismissing the idea and breaking through layers of conventionality. It encouraged her to say, "Perhaps you'd find out why Joshua's life changed after going there."

Mrs. Stanhope sniffed. "I hardly think that would happen."

"Please?" Ellie felt as if she were fighting for her future. "Just this once? I'd really like you to be there for me." *And for Josh,* she silently added.

"My goodness, but you're persistent." A long-suffering look etched itself into Mrs. Stanhope's face. "If it means that much to you, I suppose I should go, although it's against my better judgment." She bustled out. Ellie wanted to cheer.

Ellie would never forget the expression on Marvin Stanhope's face as his sister-in-law swept into the Rescue Mission. It matched her husband's and son's disbelief when she had blandly announced she planned to accompany them to hear Ellie sing. But after the first shocked moment, Marvin rose to the occasion.

"Thank you for coming." He led his guests to chairs at the front of a shabby room that smelled of cleanliness and boiling coffee. To Ellie's relief, both the room and its occupants had obviously been subject to strong soap and water. Mrs. Stanhope didn't turn a hair, even when a motley collection of unfortunates filed in and filled the chairs. Others stood at the back. It seemed as if every derelict for miles around, as well as the *Chronicle* reporter who sang Ellie's praises, had come to hear the Sierra Songbird.

Edward sat down at the old but surprisingly well-tuned piano. Ellie had carefully selected a program designed to appeal to this particular audience. "Please sing along if you know the words," she invited. At first no one except Edward and the newspaper reporter responded. Then grumbling bass and cracked baritone voices joined in on "Aura Lee," "Sweet Genevieve," "Beautiful Dreamer," "Silver Threads among the Gold," and a dozen others.

Ellie's heart swelled. Long ago in this very room, Red Fallon had met the Master because of a young man who fearlessly braved a dark alley and rescued him. Her pride in Joshua multiplied a hundredfold.

She gradually shifted from ballads to hymns. At last, Ellie picked up her guitar and signaled to Edward, who joined his parents. After singing "Amazing Grace," she struck the first notes of "It Is Well with My Soul." A quick glance into the sin-hardened faces with seeking eyes stilled her fingers. These men knew far too much of tragedy. They didn't need a song with a history of death and loss.

Ellie's heart pounded. "I'd like to end with 'The Ninety and Nine,' one of my favorite hymns." She played a single note, laid her guitar aside, and began to sing:

"There were ninety and nine that safely lay
In the shelter of the fold.
But one was out on the hills away,
Far off from the gates of gold.
Away on the mountains wild and bare.
Away from the tender Shepherd's care."

Feeling she was battling despair and hopelessness, Ellie continued her song. She saw expressions change. Dead-looking eyes sparked to life. The reporter leaned forward as if to make sure he didn't miss a note. Mrs. Stanhope brushed away tears. Her husband radiated satisfaction. Edward looked more serious than Ellie had ever seen him.

She triumphantly sang the final words:

"And the angels echoed around the throne,
'Rejoice, for the Lord brings back His own!
Rejoice, for the Lord brings back His own!' "

A great stillness fell over the room. The bubble of a huge coffeepot on a nearby stove sounded loud in Ellie's ears. Then a storm of applause reached the rafters. Ellie's tears flowed, and she stumbled to a seat.

Marvin Stanhope walked to the front. His face glowed with love. "There is greater rejoicing in heaven over one lost sheep who is returned to the fold than for all those who never go astray. Please bow your heads."

A ripple of movement crept through the audience.

Ellie could scarcely contain her feelings when Marvin said, "Tonight the Good Shepherd is seeking those who are lost. He is not out on some wild, bare mountain or in a deep valley, but here with us. Lord, if there's one in this place who is willing to follow You, let that person come forward."

After what felt like an eternity, a wizened old man shuffled to the front. "Pray for me," he said.

Ellie heard little of the prayer that followed. Her heart thudded against the walls of her chest until it seemed it would burst. Had God led her to San Francisco, not for fame and fortune, but to teach her what Joshua had learned long ago? Service to God through serving His children was what really mattered.

A few days later, Josh sat at his table, reading the excited letter from Ellie for the fifth time. It had taken that many readings to fully grasp her news. What magic had Ellie used to persuade Mother to go with her to the Rescue Mission, a place she'd sneered at for years? His heart leaped. Could it be the first step in reconciliation?

"Yoo-hoo! Preacher Josh, are you home?" a girlish voice called, interrupting Josh's fervent prayer of thanks.

Josh gritted his teeth. He'd always heard trouble came in threes. Trouble came in twos in Madera: Luther and Amy Talbot. He stepped outside. There was no way under heaven he'd allow Amy inside the parsonage unless others were present. What did she want now? She'd plagued him with invitations until his excuses had worn threadbare.

Amy flitted toward him, a vision in pale pink from parasol to slippers. Lovely, except for her cold, china blue eyes. "May we go inside? It's warm for October."

"We'll go to the church."

She pouted. "Abby Fallon's practicing on the organ. I want to talk to you alone."

Josh inwardly shuddered. "I hardly think your father would approve of that."

Amy fluttered her eyelashes and looked sly. "He doesn't have to know."

"You think anyone in Madera can do anything without being found out? Besides, I'm on trial here." He regretted the words the second they popped out.

Amy raised a delicate eyebrow. "Father won't dismiss you unless I say so."

Josh didn't trust himself to answer. He led Amy into the church, ushered her into a pew at the back, and sat down beside her. "Keep practicing," he called to Abby. "You won't bother us."

"She bothers me," Amy grumbled, then looked down at her gloved hands. "She can't hear us, can she?"

A warning bell rang in Josh's brain. "No."

Amy's eyes gleamed. "I want to ask you a question. If a girl — a young woman — wants a certain man, is it unmaidenly for her to ask him to marry her?"

Josh gaped like a fish out of water.

"Well?"

Josh found his voice and got to his feet at the same time. He purposely raised his voice, loud enough for Abby to hear. "Miss Talbot, I hope you are jesting. It would not only be unmaidenly, but improper for a young woman to ask a man to marry her."

It didn't seem to faze the bold girl. "Even when marrying her means saving the man she wants from being fired?"

Josh could barely conceal his dislike. "Absolutely. Now if you'll excuse me, I need to speak with Abby." He stepped back into the aisle, but her shrill voice followed him.

"You'll rue this day!" She elbowed her way past him and ran out of the church, bang-

238

ing the door behind her.

Josh walked to the front of the church and stared at Abby.

"What's Amy up to now?" she asked.

"That spoiled young lady thinks she can have everything she wants, including me."

Abby's giggle brought a reluctant grin. "I probably shouldn't have told you," Josh apologized.

Abby sobered, and a worried look came into her dark eyes. "I'm glad you did. Knowing Amy, you may need a witness." She rested her hands on the keyboard. "Don't forget that a woman scorned, especially one like Amy, is big trouble."

"Let's forget her and talk about the hymns for Sunday," Josh suggested. "A much more pleasant subject."

Abby nodded, but before they finished deciding on what songs best fit Josh's subject, the door slammed open. Luther Talbot stormed in with Amy right behind him.

"Reverend Stanhope, what's this I hear about you insulting my daughter?" he bellowed. "She came home in tears and refused to repeat whatever it is you said to her. You may do things differently in San Francisco, but we don't stand for such here."

Josh felt anger begin at his toes and crawl its way up. "Keep your voice down. This is the house of God." He ignored Luther's gasp and fixed his gaze on Amy's smirking face. "Tell your father the truth, or I shall."

Amy's eyes widened, and she put on an aggrieved air. "Why, Preacher Josh, whatever do you mean?"

Sickened by her pretense, Josh turned to Luther. "Mr. Talbot, is your daughter in the habit of asking men to marry her?"

Luther's jaw dropped. "What are you talking about?"

Josh didn't give an inch. "I'd hoped never to repeat our little conversation, but since Amy chooses to play innocent, you need to know what happened. I did not insult her. I did tell her it's unmaidenly and improper for a young woman to ask a man to marry her — and only after she asked. Mrs. Fallon heard what I said."

Luther grabbed his daughter by the shoulders and shook her. "Is that true?"

"I was only teasing the preacher," she whimpered. "He took it all wrong."

Josh's temper boiled over. "Was it also teasing when you asked if it would still be inappropriate if marrying her meant saving the man she wanted from being fired?"

Amy burst into sobs, freed herself, and stumbled out the open door.

Josh watched Luther's prominent Adam's

apple go up and down before the gaunt man said, "I may have been a bit hasty." He turned on his heel and marched out, his spine stiffer than a hickory walking stick.

Abby's laughter released some of Josh's fury. She rocked back and forth on the organ bench, then wiped away tears. Mirth, however, soon gave way to concern. "This isn't going to endear you to either Luther or Amy."

Josh stared at her. "It also won't improve my chances of staying on at Christ the Way." He walked out and headed for the livery stable. The best medicine for getting the Talbots and their doings out of his system was a long, hard gallop on Sultan.

TWENTY-THREE

Joshua Stanhope stared at the red-circled date on his calendar. Tomorrow, November 30, ended his six-month trial period at Christ the Way. And tomorrow he'd board the train to San Francisco.

Would he be back? The grim-faced church board had silently listened when Josh laid down his conditions for further service: freedom to serve outside the church as well as inside. But Luther Talbot's noncommittal "We'll let you know" indicated that unless God intervened, Josh would be out of a job.

A pang shot through him. "Lord, I've come to love the church and most of the people. Glad I'm getting away, though. I can hardly wait to see my family and Ellie."

Fear nibbled at his anticipation. What would he find? The girl he loved or a changed young woman?

Josh brushed the disloyal thought aside

but fought depression all the way to San Francisco. Mother had been friendly when she and Edward came to kidnap Ellie, but how did she feel now that she'd gotten what she wanted?

When the carriage reached the mansion on Nob Hill at dusk, Josh paid the driver and strode up the walk and onto the porch. He thought of the lost son who came home to his father's house from a far country, sick and uncertain of his welcome. Although Josh's circumstances differed, new understanding of the young man's feelings filled him. *Why didn't I tell my family I was coming? Father would have rushed out to greet me, just like the lost son's father,* he reflected. Josh raised and dropped the heavy knocker. The door opened.

"Senor Joshua," Maria gasped. "You are home?"

"Yes, Maria." He stepped into the brightly lit hall. "Where is the family?"

"In the drawing room." She scuttled ahead of him, talking all the way. "I do not think they are expecting you. Senorita Ellie would have told me."

Josh thanked her and pushed open the heavy drawing-room doors. Heart beating like a bass drum, he stepped inside, leaving the doors open. "Howdy, folks." *What a dunce. I haven't been home in months, and I say howdy?*

Three shocked faces turned toward him. Mother's hand flew to her throat. Edward and Father leaped up and met him halfway across the room. Father gripped Josh's hand. "Welcome home, Son."

Edward pounded on his shoulder. "Great to see you, old man. Why didn't you tell us you were coming?"

"I wanted to surprise you."

Mother's chin wobbled. "You certainly have, Joshua. I — we've missed you."

Relief threatened to buckle Josh's knees. He hurried across the costly rug and knelt beside her chair. "I've missed you too, Mother. All of you." He looked around the lavishly furnished room. "Where's Ellie — Miss Sterling?"

A rustle behind him whipped Josh around. A soft voice said, "I'm here."

Josh stared. The white-robed girl in the doorway looked like she'd stepped out of a painting. "Ellie?"

"Don't you know me?" She glided to him and held out her hand.

Josh folded it in his. "I'm not sure," he told her. "You look different —"

"Of course she looks different," his mother interrupted. "Surely you didn't expect her to look the same as when she lived on a ranch. Not that there's anything wrong with ranches," she hastily added. Her unaccustomed tact surprised Josh. Evidently Ellie wasn't the only person who had changed.

"I'm glad you've come," Ellie said.

The feel of her soft hand in his and the expression in her eyes made Josh feel better.

In the days that followed, however, he realized how much Ellie had changed. Not only in dress, but in the confident way she carried herself . . . and how she fit into city life. Josh searched in vain for the Ellie he'd fallen in love with: the girl in the yellow calico gown that made her look like a western meadowlark. Did she still exist? Or was San Francisco changing the Sierra Songbird into a society peacock?

Early one chilly morning, Josh climbed high atop a hill overlooking the Pacific Ocean. "Lord, it seems everyone at Bayview Christian expects me to come back, except Reverend Michael Yates. I no longer belong in San Francisco. I can't stay, even if it means losing Ellie — and it may. She seems so thrilled with her success here."

Josh stared unseeingly at the rolling waves breaking against the shore far below. "I feel like a man without a country. I want to go back to Madera, but surely I'd have heard if they plan to keep me." He groaned. "If they don't, how can I ask Ellie to give up all this for a preacher without a church?"

Hours later, the cold drove Josh back to the mansion on Nob Hill. Strange. After only six months, he felt more at home in the Madera parsonage than in the home where he'd been born. He raised his head and clenched his jaw, determined to corral Ellie.

So far, trying to get her alone had been futile. His opportunity came that afternoon. Edward was out and about; Father at his shipping office. After lunch, Mother retired to her room for a nap. Josh told Ellie, "We need to talk."

Her eyes darkened. "I know." She led him to the library and motioned him to a chair, as if she were the daughter of the house and he a mere guest. "How's everyone on the Diamond S?"

"Fine, but I don't want to talk about them. When are you coming back to Madera where you belong?" Josh saw her stiffen at his blunt question.

"I belong here." Ellie leaned forward. "I'm doing a great deal of good with my singing. Everyone says so."

"More than in Madera? Is singing to throngs of people more important than seeing lives changed at the hand-hewn altar in Christ the Way?"

Every trace of color fled from her face. She stared at if seeing Josh for the first time.

"Tim thinks you're settling for fool's gold instead of real gold. Has all this glitter spoiled you?" He waved at the luxury surrounding them.

The harsh words hung in the air. Ellie's eyes looked enormous. "Do you think so?"

"I don't know. I —"

A tap on the door cut into Josh's reply. He got to his feet. "Yes?"

Maria entered, holding a letter. "For you. Senor. It came this morning, but you were not here." She handed it to Josh and scurried out.

Josh glanced at the envelope. His world turned black.

Ellie slipped from her chair and came to his side. "Is it from the church board?"

"No. From Tim." He tossed her the unopened message. "He's probably blasting Luther and his buddies for getting rid of me. Here, you read it." He watched Ellie slit the envelope and unfold the single page. Tears sparkled on her lashes. She glanced down and began to laugh. "If this isn't just like Tim! No greeting, just this:

"Luther called a secret meeting of those who don't want you here. Red got wind of it. He rounded up members and a bunch of cowhands and sheepherders who like you.

"They busted into the meeting. Red up and told the board Jesus came to save folks with the gumption to admit they're sinners. He said God's love ain't s'posed to be kept locked up inside the church. You shoulda heard folks cheer!

"It shook the board up (specially when Red hinted a new board could get picked). Anyhow, they voted to let you run things your way. Hurry home before they change their minds."

Josh gave a great shout. "Well, God bless Red Fallon!" He gently grasped Ellie's shoulders. "Now that I have a job again, will you marry me, Ellie? Right away?"

Ellie clasped her hands around his arm and gazed into his face. She looked stricken. "I want to marry you, but until God lets me know my work here is done, I can't."

Josh stared down into her troubled face. The sincerity in her voice could not be ignored. "I can't argue with what you feel God is telling you to do, Ellie. Just make sure you're hearing Him right." Josh bent and kissed her upturned lips, then released her and left the room.

Ellie watched Josh go. She longed to rush after him and erase the bitter disappointment in his eyes. She could not, so she flew to her room for refuge. Her respite, however, was short lived. Just before dinner, Maria appeared.

"The senor from the newspaper is waiting to see you."

Ellie rebelled. "Tell him I can't see him."

Maria shook her head. "He said it is *muy* important."

"All right." Ellie smoothed her hair and went back to the library.

The reporter's sober countenance frightened her. "Miss Sterling, the *Chronicle* received an anonymous message today. I regret bringing it to you, but others may have also received it." He handed her a sheet of paper.

Bold black words stared up at her: *Ask the Sierra Songbird about her real father and jailbird brothers.* The page slipped to the floor. Ellie wanted to flee. Just when she thought herself over the past, a dozen malicious words had brought it all back.

"What do you want me to do with this?" the reporter asked.

An old saying came to mind. *Tell the truth and shame the devil.* "You need to hear and write the truth." Ellie saw admiration sneak into his watching eyes. "Come back this evening after I have time to talk with the Stanhopes."

He nodded and left. Ellie sank to the settee. "Lord, I dread telling them, especially Mrs. Stanhope. Well, whatever happens, I'll be free from the fear of discovery. I just hope it doesn't cause more trouble for Joshua." She went to her room and donned her prettiest dress. Somewhat calmed by the knowledge that God was still in control, she went down to dinner. When the meal ended, she quietly said, "I have something to tell you. May we go into the library, please?"

Mrs. Stanhope looked startled. "Of course." She rose and led the way. With a silent prayer for help, Ellie waited until everyone was seated in the restful room.

"The *Chronicle* received an anonymous message today," she began. "It said to ask me about my real father and brothers." She fixed her gaze on Mrs. Stanhope and told the story of Ellie Stoddard who became Ellie Sterling. She spared none of the details, even though they seemed more sordid than ever when related in this luxurious setting. Ellie watched Mrs. Stanhope's face grow

250

mottled with rage, change to disbelief, soften with compassion, and grow tight-lipped, but the older woman didn't interrupt.

Ellie ended with, "I'm sorry for the embarrassment this will cause you, but I intend to give the reporter the full story. He's coming back tonight." Her self-control broke. Tears dripped. "I wish I'd told you everything before I agreed to come here."

Mrs. Stanhope turned to Joshua and glared. "Did you know about Ellie's past?"

A steely look came into his gray eyes. "Yes, but not how bad it really was."

"And you didn't see fit to tell me."

Ellie cringed. Would this cause another rift between mother and son?

Josh's lips curved into a smile of incredible sweetness. "Stoddard or Sterling, Ellie is the most wonderful girl in the world."

"Amen," Edward put in.

"Do be quiet, Edward. This doesn't concern you."

To Ellie's dismay, he began to laugh. "Wake up, Mother. The truth is written all over Josh's face. Ellie's going to be my sister, and I couldn't be happier!"

Mrs. Stanhope pinned Ellie with a stare. "Do you love my son? Has he told your father — Mr. Sterling — that he wants to marry you?"

"Y–yes, but I haven't said I'd —"

Mrs. Stanhope went into her take-charge mode. "Then I suggest you do so at once. No one will dare cast aspersions on a future Stanhope." She stood and started toward the door. "Charles, tell the reporter to drop a hint about Joshua and Ellie in his story." To Ellie's utter amazement Mrs. Stanhope's eyes twinkled. Genuine affection lurked in their depths. "This has been a most surprising evening, but I always wanted a daughter. With a little more training, you'll do nicely, my dear."

She swept out, leaving Edward cackling like a laying hen and Ellie in a state of shock.

Mr. Stanhope quietly said, "I couldn't be more pleased, Joshua. Edward, stop laughing and come with me. Your brother and Ellie need to be alone."

The door closed behind them. Through blinding tears, Ellie saw Joshua coming toward her. The next moment she was safe in his arms.

The next issue of the *Chronicle* carried a story that Ellie considered a masterpiece:

SCURRILOUS ATTEMPT TO CLIP
SIERRA SONGBIRD'S WINGS FAILS

A vicious effort to discredit Miss Ellianna Sterling has come to naught. An anonymous message, "Ask the Sierra Songbird about her real father and jailbird brothers," aroused the ire of this justice-loving reporter. In an exclusive interview, Miss Sterling frankly stated she was born in St. Louis, Missouri, as Ellianna Stoddard and was raised in poverty. At age eleven, she and her younger brother came to live with their stepbrother and stepsister in Madera.

Matthew Sterling — owner of the largest cattle ranch in the San Joaquin Valley and married to Miss Sterling's stepsister — legally adopted Ellianna and Timothy.

While it's true that Miss Sterling's older brothers were jailed, they were soon cleared and released from the trumped-up charge.

Cowards who refuse to sign messages need not send them to the *Chronicle* — especially to this reporter. Nay, go ahead and send them. They make a perfect lining for the bottom of birdcages.

On a happier note, tittle-tattle has it that wedding bells may someday ring for Joshua Stanhope and the Sierra Songbird.

When asked about the rumor, the elder Stanhopes and their son Edward simply smiled and looked pleased.

TWENTY-FOUR

San Francisco took up arms in Ellie's defense after the scorching *Chronicle* article appeared. Letters to the editor poured in. Then the enterprising reporter tracked down the envelope that brought the anonymous letter.

It was postmarked Madera.

"Amy Talbot probably wrote it," Josh said. "The *Fresno Expositor* and the *Madera Tribune* both ran the article and mentioned the postmark. Eventually the culprit will be exposed, punishment enough."

Ellie agreed. She knew only too well how it felt to be the subject of gossip.

The next day, she hid tears and told Josh good-bye. "Your visit was too short."

"I need to get back to Christ the Way." Josh brushed away the lone tear Ellie couldn't hold back. "It's only a few weeks until Christmas." He kissed her ring finger. "I'll have something special for you when you come home."

"All I want is you."

Josh's eyes twinkled. "You already have that!" A quick kiss, and he was gone.

The following morning, Ellie sat by her window and stared out into rain mixed with sleet. Tree branches bent and shivered in the wind. Ellie already missed Josh. Homesickness for the Diamond S and the promontory where she'd spent so many happy hours overwhelmed her. She longed for rolling rangeland and canyons instead of tall buildings and cobblestone streets. For clear, crisp mornings untouched by fog.

Ellie wrapped herself into a colorful shawl Solita had made. The red, white, and emerald green reminded Ellie of Christmas. She closed her eyes and thought of last year's program at Christ the Way. Everyone had brought gifts to the altar. Not gold, frankincense, or myrrh, but food, clothing, treasured toys, and money — some from those who had little to spare — for a family who had lost their home and possessions to fire.

Ellie hadn't written even one song since she'd come to San Francisco. Now words tumbled into her mind. She snatched writing materials and let them pour out:

Tell me, kind shepherds, when you came to

the manger,
What gifts did you bring to the new little
    stranger
Who quietly lay asleep on the hay?
We had no fine gifts on that glorious night
When the fields were ablaze with a
    heavenly light.
So our voices we raised in worship and
    praise.
Tell me, oh Wise Men who came from afar,
What did you bring when you followed the
    Star,
And found Him that day in the house where
    He lay?
Gold, frankincense, myrrh
From far distant lands.
We bowed down in wonder and kissed His
    small hands.
Tell me, good people, what gifts do you
    bring,
To the Savior who loves us; the King of all
    kings?
Will you open your hearts and invite Him to
    stay —
Or, like the innkeeper, turn Him away?
Or, like the innkeeper, turn Him away?"

The perfect title came to mind: "Ballad
for a King." Ellie bowed her head. "Lord,
You've given me the gift of song. I'm trying

to use it for You, but I want to do something more to honor Your Son. I just don't know what."

"Forgive."

The word pierced Ellie's soul. She let tears flow while she took a fresh sheet of paper and wrote: *I forgive you, Pa. Ellie.* She placed it in an envelope that she sealed and addressed. Then she tucked her poem inside her dress to nestle above her heart and ran downstairs.

Warmed by the poem's presence, Ellie buried her letter among the others to be posted. Her heart pumped with joy. "Lord, I haven't felt this clean since I was baptized in the stream on the Diamond S. Pa probably won't reply, but I'm free." She danced upstairs and into her room.

Mrs. Stanhope sat by the window. Her hands nervously pleated and smoothed a fold of her costly skirt. "Ellie, I have to tell you something."

Dread shot through Ellie. "Is Josh hurt?"

"No, it's something else. Would it break your heart to spend Christmas here?"

Ellie's knees gave way. She dropped to the bed. "Why?"

"Governor Markham has asked for a private musicale at our home. It's your chance of a lifetime." Mrs. Stanhope sighed.

"Unfortunately, the governor and his wife are only free on Christmas Eve."

Ellie's dreams for the holidays fled. How could she say no when Mrs. Stanhope had done so much for her? Ellie had grown to love Joshua's mother since being welcomed to the family. She'd also seen the older woman slowly become a more understanding person.

"You don't have to stay." Josh's mother rose and patted Ellie's hand. "Pray about it and do what you feel is right. We won't hold it against you if you go home as planned." She frowned. "I've known Henry Markham for years and have already told him you might not be available. He should have picked a better time." She marched out.

Ellie stared after her. The unexpected advice to pray and willingness to leave the decision in Ellie's hands were more effective than pleading or reminders of duty. "Lord, how will everyone at home feel, especially Joshua?" Her throat constricted. "Besides, if I stay here, I'll be so disappointed I won't be able to sing."

She stood and started for the door, intending to tell Mrs. Stanhope she couldn't give up her plans. Yet a feeling that more than Governor Markham's whim hung on her decision stopped her. The tumult in her soul gradually stilled. She bowed her head and whispered through her unhappiness, "I'll stay."

"Perhaps you can go home for New Year's," Mr. Stanhope said when Ellie announced her decision, but Edward shook his head.

"Sorry, Ellie." He looked genuinely regretful. "The only time we could reserve the Palace Hotel is on New Year's Day. I know you sing for more than money, but this performance will bring in an incredible sum. It will also be your largest audience."

Ellie could barely hide her distress. She couldn't afford to turn down such an opportunity. She'd had to dip into her slow-growing savings too many times. She also thought about the spectators. The rich as well as those at the Rescue Mission needed to hear the gospel. Perhaps one among them would be touched by her singing. "All right, but after that, I need to go home."

"Speaking of going, we need to go practice," Edward said. "How about right now?"

"Of course."

The afternoon sped by. Mrs. Stanhope's news and Ellie's turmoil had driven away all thought of her poem until she went up to change for dinner. She removed her dress and shook it. No page fell to the rug. Ellie searched her room and retraced her steps from earlier that day without success. "A servant must have found and disposed of it," she decided. "It's foolish to inquire about a scribbled piece of paper. I can write it again." The hustle and bustle of the upcoming holidays, however, pushed it from her mind. So much to do. So many places to go.

By Christmas Eve, all Ellie wanted was to lie on her bed, look out into the star-filled sky, and think of the Christmas Star that shone close to two thousand years earlier. Instead, she donned a new yellow silk gown and filled the drawing room with music. Governor Markham, his wife, and the other guests called her back for encore after encore.

Free at last, Ellie stole away from the adoring crowd and escaped to her bedroom. The contrast between the merriment and the first Christmas saddened her. "Father, does anyone here except me think of the humble stable where Your Son was born?" She pressed her face to the window, glad for its cool touch. "Joshua is right. I've been dazzled by the glitter. Jesus said, 'Where your treasure is, there will your heart be also.' Well, my heart and treasure are in Madera. Lord, how long must I stay here?"

Discouraged and lonely, she cried herself to sleep.

New Year's came and went. Ellie surpassed herself at the Palace Hotel concert, but once the excitement of performing in such a splendid place died, she grew restless. God showed no sign of delivering her. "I'll stay because I feel it's Your will," she prayed, "but it would be easier if I knew why." Heart heavy with unshed tears, even the familiar admonition, *"Trust Me,"* failed to bring comfort.

A few days later, Mrs. Stanhope summoned Ellie to the library. Ellie had never seen her in such a state. "Ellie, we have wronged you."

"It's my fault." Edward held out a printed piece of sheet music that read: "Ballad for a King," *by Ellianna Sterling. Music by Ludwig Karl and Edward Stanhope.*

Ellie blinked. "What — how . . . ?"

Edward paced the floor. "I found your poem on the staircase and showed it to a composer friend. Ludwig said it had worth. We set it to music."

Ellie clapped her hands. "That's wonderful!" She turned her attention to Letitia. "But why did you say you've wronged me?"

Tears spilled down the older woman's

face. She shook her head and didn't reply.

Edward stopped pacing. "Mother was thrilled when I told her. She wanted to rush to you with the news. So did I — until I realized what it meant. Ludwig predicts it will bring you large royalties and open the door for you to write other songs."

Ellie felt she stood at the edge of a mystery. "I still don't understand."

"You've been good for all of us, especially me." Edward's eyes glistened. "Ludwig wants me to continue as his collaborator."

"What exciting news," Ellie cried, but Edward shuffled his feet and looked uncomfortable.

"It's only part of the story. This is the only printed copy of your song. I made Ludwig promise to keep it secret for a time. I also selfishly convinced Mother that we needed to keep you here as long as we could — even though Josh had slipped and mentioned your dream of helping your brother. Don't you see, Ellie? This opens the way for you to go home. You can write anywhere."

Ellie's brain whirled. "Why are you telling me this now?"

He looked ashamed. "You'll have to sign a contract for the song to be published. Anyway, Mother insisted you be told. She will tell you why."

Mrs. Stanhope dabbed at her eyes and sent Ellie a pleading look. "I wanted to believe Edward was right. I hoped your being here might bring Joshua home, even though deep in my heart I knew it wouldn't happen. Remember the night at the Rescue Mission when you sang 'The Ninety and Nine'?"

Ellie thought of Josh's mother brushing away tears. "Yes."

Mrs. Stanhope sniffled. "I can't explain it, but the story of Jesus leaving the flock and going to help the lost sheep reminded me of Joshua when he said he was going to Madera."

Ellie couldn't have been more shocked if the roof had opened and a meteorite had hurled into the quiet library. Her heart hammered with understanding. God had led her to San Francisco for unknown reasons, but none as important as this.

Mrs. Stanhope continued. "After Edward showed me 'Ballad for a King,' I made a copy of it. I didn't tell him, but I read it again and again, especially the last stanza:

"Tell me, good people, what gifts do you
      bring,
To the Savior who loves us; the King of all
      kings?

Will you open your hearts and invite Him to
    stay —
Or, like the innkeeper, turn Him away?
Or, like the innkeeper, turn Him away?"

"I've always tried to do right and help others, but I've realized I'm just like the innkeeper." Letitia raised her tearstained face. "No more. This morning, I gave Jesus a gilt-edged invitation to live in my heart."

Ellie felt torn between the desire to weep for joy and shout with laughter. How like Mrs. Stanhope to surrender her life to the Lord in such a manner! Ellie sprang from her chair, ran across the room, and knelt at the woman's side. "I am so happy!" She clasped Letitia's hands in her own. "This is the greatest gift you could give to God, me, and" — her lips trembled — "to Joshua."

"He already knows. I sent a telegram an hour ago." Mrs. Stanhope turned to Edward with a look of undeniable longing. "Now if only —"

Edward raised his hands in mock protest. "Don't preach, Mother. One minister in the family is plenty." But Ellie noticed an unaccustomed softness in his attitude. Her heart throbbed. Perhaps someday Edward would —

"Trust Me."

265

The words rang in Ellie's heart. *Lord, my work here is finished. Although I've often been rebellious, I can say like the Apostle Paul, I have fought a good fight, finished my course, and kept the faith. Now I'm free to fly home to Madera — and Joshua.*

Valentine's Day 1893
Sunlight poured through the windows of Christ the Way Church. It bathed the couple standing before the altar in radiance rivaled by Preacher Josh's face when he glanced down at Ellie. Her spirit rushed out to him. What had she ever done to deserve such happiness?

"With this ring I thee wed."

Joshua's vow touched Ellie's soul. She looked into his shining gray eyes, then at the ring he placed on her waiting finger. Her heart soared. It had been a long, hard flight before the Sierra Songbird found priceless treasure: a golden circle without beginning or end . . . just like her heavenly Father's love.

Dear Readers,

History really does repeat itself. When I finished writing *Romance Rides the Range,* book one of my western series, I was planted (in spirit) on the Diamond S Ranch near Madera, California, in the 1880s. I couldn't bear to say good-bye and move on.

The same thing happened with book two, *Romance Rides the River.* Tangled, unexplored trails in the beautiful San Joaquin Valley and surrounding countryside lured me. Characters, old and new, grabbed me and clamored for a place in the sun. *Romance at Rainbow's End* is my response to my true-to-life "book friends" who refused to be silent.

This title — like *Romance Rides the Range* and *Romance Rides the River* — recognizes God's unfailing love for all of His children, particularly for the "mavericks" who stray from His presence. May it serve as a reminder that we are branded with the name Jesus Christ and are called to round up others and establish His ownership.

God bless you all,
Colleen

I love to hear from my readers! You may correspond with me by writing:

267

Colleen L. Reece
Author Relations
PO Box 721
Uhrichsville, OH 44683

ABOUT THE AUTHOR

Colleen L. Reece was born and raised in a small western Washington logging town. She learned to read by kerosene lamplight and dreamed of someday writing a book. God has multiplied Colleen's "someday" book into more than 140 titles that have sold six million copies. Colleen was twice voted Heartsong Presents' Favorite Author and later inducted into Heartsong's Hall of Fame. Several of her books have appeared on the CBA bestseller list.